THE ATHO[illegible]

Alex Roddie is a writer [illegible]
fiction. After studying Com[illegible]
East Anglia in Norwich, he [illegible]
the Clachaig Inn, Glen C[illegible]
climbed extensively and n[illegible] writing about his adventures. After founding the popular winter climbing blog, *Glencoe Mountaineer*, he began working on his first novel, *The Only Genuine Jones*—a process aided by his practical research into Victorian winter climbing equipment and techniques. He now lives in Lincolnshire with his partner Hannah, and is currently obsessed with the late 1840s.

Praise for *The Atholl Expedition:*

"A book for anyone who loves wild places and cracking good yarns … I love the fictional/philosophical mix of Alex's writing and he has a wonderful eye for the unseen."

Outdoor blogger Alistair Young

"His research into this period is thorough and faultless and his writing contains some beautiful descriptions of the landscape of the Cairngorms which reveal his own love of the mountains. This novel written in the style of the period will transport you to the mountains and glens of the Highlands where a dramatic chase takes place with unexpected consequences. A great little read."

Outdoor blogger John Burns

"I have always admired the author's approach to descriptive writing. It's not easy to do without sounding florid but his descriptions of storms, or of the mountains themselves, are studies in the careful choice of words. I love this style and I very much enjoyed the adventure story aspect of this book."

Book blogger Kath Middleton

BY THE SAME AUTHOR

The Only Genuine Jones

Crowley's Rival

THE

ATHOLL EXPEDITION

Being the first volume of

ALPINE DAWN

by

ALEX RODDIE

WWW.ALEXRODDIE.COM

M M X I V

THE ATHOLL EXPEDITION

Published in 2014 by FeedARead Publishing

www.feedaread.com

www.catherinespeakman.co.uk

Cover design and maps by the author

Cover image by Albert Bierstadt – *A Storm in the Rocky Mountains, Mt. Rosalie* (1866)

Victorian clip art from

www.thegraphicsfairy.com

First Paperback Edition

British Library CIP

A CIP catalogue record for this title is available from the British Library

This book is dedicated to

JAMES DAVID FORBES

1809 – 1868

Mapper of unmapped regions and tireless explorer of the mountain realm.

We turned and surveyed, with a stronger sense of sublimity than before, the desolation by which we were surrounded, and became still more sensible of our isolation from human dwellings, human help, and human sympathy.

JAMES FORBES, 1843

This is a work of speculative fiction. While some of my characters are based on historical figures, I have changed aspects of their personalities and events in their lives to fit my story. Other characters are entirely fictional. Please see the Historical Notes for more details about the changes I have made for the purposes of my story.

All events after the 21st of August, 1847, are imaginary.

CONTENTS

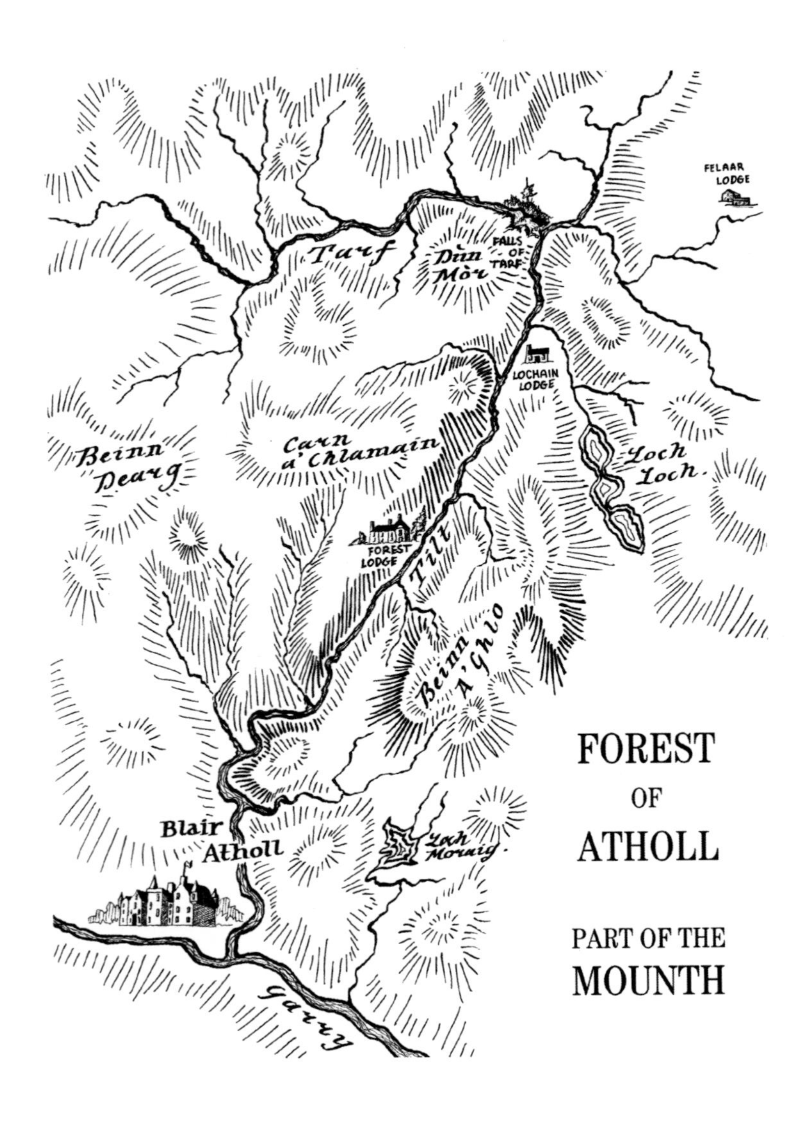
FELAAR LODGE
Tarf
Dùn Mòr
FALLS OF TARF
LOCHAIN LODGE
Carn a' Chlamain
Beinn Dearg
Loch Loch
FOREST LODGE
Tilt
Beinn A'Ghlo
Blair Atholl
Loch Moraig
Garry
FOREST OF ATHOLL
PART OF THE MOUNTH

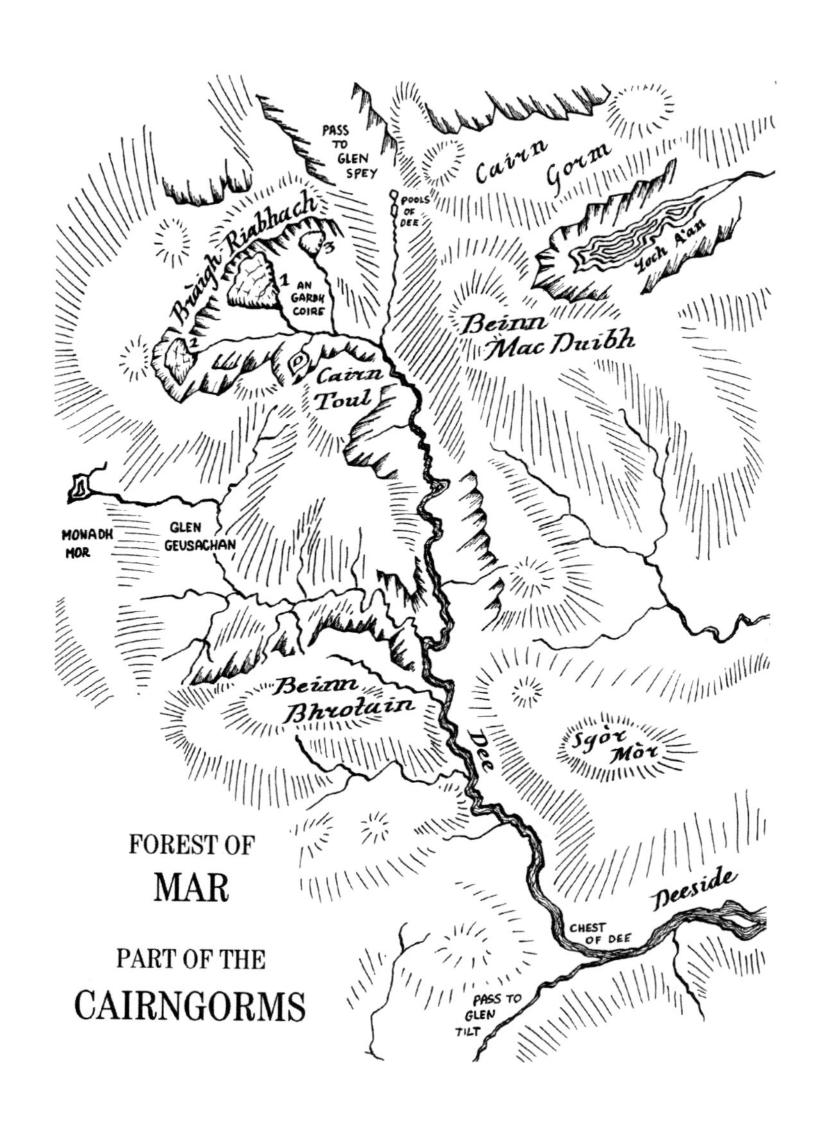

FOREST OF
MAR

PART OF THE
CAIRNGORMS

The determination to conquer is often the talisman to success.

JAMES FORBES, 1843

CHAPTER I
THE CHALLENGE

August 1847

PROFESSOR JAMES FORBES WOKE GRADUALLY, marvelling at the absence of pain. He lay there on the lawn without opening his eyes, enjoying the sounds of a summer afternoon in the Highlands: the music of a bumblebee, the distant complaints of cattle, the laughter of his children in the house. He breathed in the fragrance of heather. Beneath his hand lay a book, abandoned on the grass.

What a distressing dream. As on so many occasions before, he had been locked in a bitter struggle with his old scientific adversary, Agassiz, the Swiss upstart who had stolen his work and robbed his career of the distinction he deserved.

He opened his eyes and the pain returned, gnawing like a rat in his bowels.

'James! Where are you?'

His wife's shout cut through the peace of the afternoon. He sat upright, feeling dizzy from the exertion. *I should not have fallen asleep…*

'In the garden,' he replied weakly.

Alicia walked through the dappled light and shade of the orchard, lifting her skirts out of the grass. Her hands were streaked with flour and her face wore that determined expression Forbes had seen many times during the course of their marriage. Something had happened to disrupt the order of her household.

She stopped at the apple tree and, unconsciously, a hand went to the swell in her belly where their unborn child was growing. A smile came to her despite her agitation. Forbes loved that fleeting smile: it was meant for nobody but him, came unbidden, and made her face glow with beauty.

Then she remembered she was supposed to be annoyed, and shook her head with an unconvincing stern expression.

'How did you manage to sneak that book out here without my noticing? You are supposed to be resting, not studying! The physicians—'

'—Don't know what they are talking about,' Forbes finished for her, smiling back to show he was not entirely in earnest. 'I cannot abide this enforced idleness. I am a Professor, not a gentleman of leisure.'

'But your health is fragile, my dear. I wish you would not fight it.' She reached down and cradled his head with her arm. Her touch was very gentle. 'When you are ready, come inside for a moment. We have a visitor.'

He frowned. 'A visitor? All the way out here in the country?'

'One of your students has been adventuring over the mountains and is very tired—a Mr Carr, I believe. He is taking tea and telling stories to the children.' She looked back with a teasing smile. 'He mentioned a glacier.'

* * *

Forbes paused at the open doorway to impress the scene upon his memory. Nowadays his sense of mortality was very keen, and he took every opportunity to remember the good moments as they came. It was his way of fighting the moments of hopelessness when he drew back into himself and looked only to the past, unable to see any promise in the future.

He knew he would not live to be an old man. The chronic illness from which he suffered, started by a bout of gastric fever several years ago, was gradually ruining his health and his strength, robbing him of the ability to do the things he loved. Every moment was to be savoured.

His two young girls, Eliza and Williamina, lay sprawled on the chequered carpet that did not quite fit the floor it attempted to cover. This was their first summer at Eastertyre, the cottage in Strathtay, and they delighted in every aspect of life away from Edinburgh: fishing in the river, climbing trees, picnics in the garden, even walks up the nearby hill when Papa felt well enough. Forbes did not believe in keeping his girls indoors like other parents did. He was an outdoors man himself, always had been, and the years when women were expected to be little more than talking ornaments were receding into the past. He wanted his children to be well-rounded individuals, capable of offering more than just good lineage to their future husbands.

Now Alicia was expecting another child. His little clan was growing, and he could not be more proud.

Ewan Carr sat on the armchair by the fireplace, knapsack and spiked pole on the floor beside him, blistered feet curling their toes in a basin of water. He gulped down mouthfuls of tea in between recounting his tale to the enthralled children.

'And then I heard the monster!' Carr said with a dramatic flourish. The girls gasped.

'The monster?' Williamina said from behind her hands.

'They say he haunts the hills of Glen Dee, howling at night and causing all manner of accidents to befall travellers. The Bodach, they call him. I spied his lair through a gap in the clouds, a terrible corrie filled up with snow and ice.'

'But it is summer,' said Eliza, the older and less credulous of the sisters. 'Surely there cannot still be snow.'

'The Cairngorm mountains are capped with snow all year round.'

Forbes chose that moment to step into the room, and his daughters sat upright, smoothing down their dresses and giggling.

Carr smiled. By habit he was an energetic fellow, even exuberant, but the stresses of his long journey had knocked some of the punch out of him. He had the sort of face that people were just starting to call old-fashioned: clean shaven (more or less; a few days in the wild will dishevel the most cultured man) with a mass of sandy hair, curly and sprouting in all directions; classically handsome, with a strong bone structure but delicate eyebrows. He had the look that, thirty years ago, men of fashion would have laboured for hours every morning to achieve. To Carr the dishevelled look came naturally.

He was, in short, the sort of fellow that ladies of a certain age referred to as "such a nice young man"—although Forbes had heard rumours of rakish behaviour.

'Professor, how good it is to see you!' The youngster's carefree smile faded a little. 'You are looking well.'

'That is a lie, but I thank you for it.' Forbes sat opposite the young man. 'Girls, go and play outside in the garden. Your Papa has important business to discuss with our guest.'

Eliza and Williamina left only after assurances that the young man would continue his story later on. The Professor took a good look at his former student. He looked exhausted after a stomp through the nearby Cairngorms. Forbes, who felt increasingly confined in the pleasant boredom of Eastertyre, was just as impatient for stories as his children.

'It looks like you have been on quite an adventure,' he remarked.

A transformation came over the young man. He shuddered and slumped forward in his chair, cradling his head in his hands.

'Dear God, sir! What a trying time I have had!' He remained motionless for a moment, then looked up, haggard and weary. 'Forgive me. I tried my best to entertain the children—they are delightful girls—but I'm quite worn out. I am very much obliged to your wife for taking me in. I … I would appreciate a drop of something stronger than tea.'

Forbes felt uneasy with the idea of giving Carr alcohol at this o'clock, but perhaps a little for medicinal purposes might be allowed.

'I have some whisky in the cabinet.'

After Forbes administered some of the *uisge beatha* of the district, and made sure with his wife that they would not be disturbed for half an hour, Carr began to recount his tale.

* * *

'I first conceived of a voyage through the Cairngorms and the Mounth after attending your lecture on the natural history of the Highlands. A little research of my own revealed that these mountains, while well known to the folk who work the land, have not been looked at by men of science, beyond a few brief incursions to collect plant specimens and so on. Also, to be quite truthful, I have lately suffered a little pecuniary embarrassment (cards, you know) and it occurred to me that I needed an adventure to take my mind off things.'

His smile looked a trifle strained, Forbes thought, and he wondered how bad this pecuniary embarrassment might be. Carr had borrowed money from the Professor more than once before.

With a breezy wave of the hand Carr dismissed any comment Forbes may have wished to make before he had the opportunity to make it.

'I departed from Fettercairn about two weeks ago, traversing the length of Glen Esk before striking out into the heart of the range. A local guide accompanied me at first, but upon hearing I wished to visit the glens of Atholl and Mar he babbled about some mythical creature said to haunt Glen Dee and left me after only a few days. He took the bulk of the food with him, and the pony, but I was given new provisions by the tenants of a hunting lodge and decided to continue.

'I found myself on the summit of Beinn MacDhuibh three days ago. The morning was foggy, and it seemed to me that as I tramped through the mist I was being followed by somebody at a great distance. I fancied I could hear echoes, or muffled shouts perhaps. I don't mind telling you, Professor, that in my hungry and weakened condition it put the fear of God into me. All that stuff about monsters suddenly didn't seem so foolish.'

Forbes chuckled and rubbed his hands together. 'My boy, you are not the first man to be disturbed by some unexpected phenomenon of nature.'

'At the time it was very convincing. Anyway, as I told the children, the clouds parted and for a full minute I witnessed a scene I never thought I would see outside the Alps: it was a glacier, clear as day, on the flank.'

A glacier!

Forbes felt his hands tighten involuntarily on the arms of his chair. A tremor ran through his body. For years he had studied glaciers and glaciation, and it had become a passion as well as a career. To discover a glacier here, in Scotland, would be tremendously exciting—and might go some way towards alleviating the boredom that was creeping up on him day by day. He could relive his glory days of 1842 and '43 when he had spent months on the ice, conducting experiments in the name of science and feeling like the most fortunate man on Earth. How he missed those long days with staff in hand and the wind in his hair!

Perhaps this is what his career needed: a new discovery, some defining moment to bring him back to the forefront of his field. The bitter years of feud with Agassiz had done too much damage, and he was not young or strong enough to start again. He needed a swift victory. The scientific world had to be reminded that James Forbes was the leading authority on glaciers.

But it could not be a glacier, surely?

'It was probably just a snow patch,' he said in an even tone, to mask his excitement.

Carr shook his head. 'I know a snow patch when I see one. I've just spent two weeks wading through the damn things. No, sir, this was a glacier all right, complete with bergschrund and crevasses. It was located in the deep glen between Cairn Toul and Bràigh Riabhach.'

Those names meant nothing to Forbes. He had traversed the Cairngorms from north to south once before, but it was a vast range, poorly understood by everyone except the foresters and ghillies who worked the estates. No accurate maps of the district existed and sometimes the same mountain might be called two different names by people living in different glens.

'Draw me a sketch map,' Forbes commanded. 'I'll find you some paper and a pen.'

Carr drew in hurried, bold strokes, conjuring up a rough depiction of the mountainous realm to the north: close by the sprawling area of glens and rolling hills known as the Mounth, and further north still, the grand heights of the Cairngorms. West of Beinn MacDuibh lay a rugged landscape of cliffs and corries, and—if Carr's interpretation was to be believed—a small glacier which had somehow survived through the aeons. Although his scientific training demanded scepticism, Forbes wanted to believe in it. A more primitive part of him, his soul perhaps, felt the thrill of the wild deep in his bones, relished the cutting wind on the heights, responded in some primeval way to the roar of a stag. That part of his mind could be moved to tears by a sunset. He had always been a Romantic deep down.

Yes, he wanted to believe that, somewhere out there, a Scottish glacier had survived.

'It's difficult to get to,' Carr was saying. 'The Atholl glens are policed by the Duke's foresters. I was lucky to escape with my life.' He said that last line with a degree of relish.

Forbes snapped out of his daydream. 'The Duke of Atholl? What does he care about the odd traveller?'

'Poachers are ravaging the estates, apparently, and the landowners are taking no chances. After coming down from the plateau I met up with a group of university men who happened to be in the district … botanists, actually. I expect you know Professor Balfour. He wished to inspect Glen Tilt with a few students and agreed that I could join him. Well, we were denied access to Glen Tilt.'

'Denied access? How?'

'By every means available to the Duke's men. We were at first threatened, then pursued and chased by deerhounds.

The foresters who patrol Glen Tilt are vicious brutes. Warning shots were fired.'

Now Forbes understood why Carr looked so exhausted. 'But why?'

'The Duke is, shall we say, enthusiastic about preventing poaching on his land. I don't mind telling you that I have taken a dislike to the man.' Carr drained his glass of whisky and smiled confidently at the Professor. 'Call me mad if you like, but I'm going out into the Atholl glens again. Balfour wishes to have another look at Glen Tilt, and I like the idea of defying the Duke after the fright he has given us. This time we shall not be seen.'

Forbes frowned. He did not like Carr's gleeful tone.

'I'd not advise that, my boy. You have done what you came here to do, and thanks to providence alone have avoided arrest, from what you tell me.'

'I … look, damn it, I don't have much to go home to at the moment, all right?' Carr's smile did not waver, but now it had a nervous quality to it.

Forbes started to reply but his words were choked by a coughing fit.

Carr looked concerned. 'Forgive me, sir. I have intruded on your peace and quiet. Your wife said you are very ill.'

Forbes laughed, but a sudden stab of agony made him stop and clutch a hand to his side. 'I'm … fine. Or at least I would be if I had a little more freedom. Sometimes I think the inactivity is what is killing me, not the illness.'

* * *

Many miles distant, at the far northern border of the Atholl estate, two of the Duke's gamekeepers were making ready for a journey.

Duncan McAdie kissed his mother on the forehead as he left the house. Gail McAdie smiled: the careworn expression of a woman resigned to a life of hard work and scant reward, and yet she carried her burdens without complaint. Duncan wished he was as stoic as his mother.

'Make sure you're there by dark or the Bodach will get you.'

'Aye, *màthair*. Dinnae fret. We're only going as far as Blair.'

A glance into the sky, and a sniff of the humid air, told him bad weather was coming. Those high wispy clouds foretold rain and a strengthening wind from the east. Lochain Lodge was built on a spur of ground between two burns: protected from the worst of the weather, reason would suggest, and yet his father had been forced to partially rebuild the property ten years ago after a particularly severe storm. This was a bad place to be caught out by the weather. It was the fate of the Highland forester to live in such a place for most of the year.

Lochain Lodge was the smallest and oldest of the Duke's hunting lodges, now considered too mean to serve its original purpose; consequently it had been turned into lodgings for estate servants many years ago. Consisting of a simple rectangular building, heated by a fire and lit by candles, it leaked in the summer and was threatened by avalanches in the winter.

His father, Alec McAdie, was loading up one of the ponies by the stone wall next to the burn. The pony (Duncan's favourite, a brown mare called Floraidh) dipped her head to the fountain and took a gulp, then tossed her head, spraying McAdie with droplets.

'Stop that, girl,' McAdie murmured, and the pony obeyed.

Duncan wondered if now was the right time to tell his father he wanted to leave Glen Tilt.

The question had been building within him for the last year, but he had not found the opportunity. Always his father had a long list of things for him to do: trek to Blair for supplies, nurse an injured dog, melt lead for rifle balls, repair the roof. Perhaps also he had been putting off the final decision. Despite the isolation and the sense of life passing him by, he knew nothing beyond this lonely and barren place.

This had not always been an empty landscape. His mother used to tell him stories of the olden days when Glen Tilt had been alive with crofts and families. The 4th Duke, a hated man who ruled from Blair Castle but cared nothing for the people, had evicted many of the crofters to create the vast deer forest that existed here today: a forest without trees, a haunted landscape of ruins and mile upon mile of windswept heather, trodden only by the stags and the rich men who came here to shoot them.

A few midges danced their infernal dance around his head, smelling fresh blood. He heard the high-pitched whine as one flew past his ear. It landed on his chin and started to feast, a tiny pinprick of life. He swatted it without a second thought and reflected that he certainly would not miss the Highland bloodsuckers.

'Pass me the rifles!'

McAdie's harsh order brought Duncan back to his senses. He passed the guns to his father, who checked over the locks, packed them in oilcloths, and loaded them onto the pony with the rest of the gear.

'Why are we still living in Lochain Lodge?'

The question slipped out before Duncan knew it had formed in his mind, and McAdie turned to regard his only son with a frown. McAdie was probably no older than fifty—nobody knew for certain—yet his face had weathered to resemble the mountains from which he eked out his living. The craggy mass of his beard was the same colour as the granite outcrops that protruded from the heather and gave shelter to the deer of the Atholl estate. Only his eyes seemed alive, alternating in their expression between anger and a sullen resentment. He seldom seemed to have time for any other emotion these days.

'Ye already ken the answer to that, laddie.'

His tone was remarkably calm.

'Maybe I'd like to hear you say it.'

His father returned to his work and steadfastly refused to look at him. The suppressed shame and disappointment was tangible. They both knew the unspoken question behind Duncan's words: *Why, after all these years, have you never been promoted?*

McAdie turned back to his son with thunder in his eyes.

'Ye'd do well to concentrate on your work and stop wi' idle thoughts!'

This conversation had happened before, and always it ended the same way. Duncan had long ago resigned himself to the fact that his father would never speak openly and honestly about it. As he grew up he found his father's attitude more and more difficult to bear. Where was his ambition, his drive, his curiosity?

But I am a young man! Duncan wanted to shout at his father. *I'm twenty years old and I have lived in this lonely place all of my life. I need something more!*

'Perhaps it's time I left,' he ventured. 'I need to be my own man.'

McAdie looked at his son with incredulity. 'Have ye lost your wits, laddie? How am I supposed to manage without ye at a time like this?'

'But—'

'Enough! The stalking season is upon us and I cannae spare you. That is all I have to say.'

Duncan made a face at his father's turned back. *I will get away from here and make a real life for myself,* he vowed. *I will not suffer the same disappointment as my father.*

* * *

Carr left Eastertyre after only a few hours of rest, insistent that his appointment with Balfour could not be missed. Forbes tried to discourage his student from heading back into the Mounth after such an ordeal, but Carr's boisterous spirit rallied with liberal application of whisky and food. He was keen to return to the Atholl glens and use what he had learned to help Balfour avoid the dangers of the Duke's reserve.

Forbes found that he could not settle after his student had gone, could not sit and enjoy his books in peace. Alicia watched him with a frown as he paced up and down the garden, Carr's sketch map in one hand, trying to make up his mind whether or not this "glacier" was worth investigating. Everything seemed to irritate him: the pleas of his children to come and play, or look at some wild creature they had found in the long grass; even the birdsong he had once found so calming now grated on his nerves.

This could be one of the most significant discoveries of my career waiting to be made—or it could be nothing at all.

He had never been a heavy sleeper, but now he woke three or four times that night, brain alive with activity and questions—always a hundred questions begging to be answered. How could a glacial mass have survived when every other glacier in Scotland had died thousands of years ago? Could it simply be a large semi-permanent snow patch seamed with glide cracks which Carr had mistaken, in his hungry and frightened condition, for genuine crevasses?

The only way to be certain was to examine it up close. Only the presence of steady downhill movement, and the characteristic veined structure Forbes had discovered in 1842, would confirm the theory.

The ache in his gut grew worse. He found himself coughing and gasping for air, and the ever-present headache was sometimes accompanied by flashes of colour and a persistent howling in his ears. Emotional agitation had always been bad for him, and now he was decidedly agitated. The doctors always recommended rest and a course of physic that made him want to vomit, but he knew deep down that his soul craved freedom above all other things.

A day after Carr's arrival, Alicia came into his study and closed the door silently behind her. Forbes could see her reflection in the window: a slight figure, modestly dressed. Every time he saw her Forbes thanked Providence that his life had been graced by such an angel.

Without turning to face her, Forbes could tell that his wife had been crying.

'James, you must put an end to this obsession.'

He straightened his papers on the desk before rising, not without a little difficulty. Alicia's expression was carefully neutral.

'I thought you understood the kind of man I am when you married me.'

'Is it so wrong of me to wish you could rest for six months of the year? Do you not realise how little we see of you during the lecturing season? The children are growing up quickly, James, and what of our new baby? What of your condition? We will not get these years back.'

She said those last words in a choked voice.

He thought carefully before replying. Alicia had never admonished him before for this reason, and now he felt like a bad husband and a worse father. Of course he felt guilty for even thinking about leaving her during the pregnancy, but she had always been stronger than he, and the previous two births had passed without complication; besides, the baby was not due for several months. A governess and a maid lodged at Eastertyre with them. He was satisfied she would come to no harm if he were to be away for a few days.

How can I explain to her how torn in two I feel?

'I'm sorry.' He drew her to his chest and held her tightly, kissing her neck. 'If you only knew how haunted I feel. The wide world out there, Alicia … the work left unfinished! Such wonders can hardly be conceived. I have been blessed.'

She felt rigid in his arms. 'A loving family is blessing enough for most men.'

'You know that I am not like most men.'

'It's true that you see the world differently.' She sighed. 'I don't understand you, and I wish I did.'

He held her at arm's length, looked into her eyes, acknowledged the pain and the confusion he saw there. Those feelings hurt, but he could not resist the forces that moved him.

'Would you want a husband who turns down the chance to improve himself and the world? Would you ever respect me again if I let Agassiz win?'

She pointedly ignored his mention of Agassiz. 'The strain could kill you.'

He stroked her hair and chuckled. 'I'm tougher than I look. Do you think I would go if I really thought I couldn't do it?'

He held her for a minute longer. Alicia understood him perfectly well; her complaints were simply the distress of a frightened soul who loved her husband and was terrified of a future without him. Forbes had come to terms with his own mortality, but his wife clung to the empty promises of doctors who understood nothing. It was simply a matter of time now: months or perhaps years.

'I will only be gone for a few days, God willing; a week at the most. Don't worry, my love.'

* * *

Duncan had never visited Blair Castle before. They left Floraidh in the care of the ostler, who took her to the stables to mingle with the fine hunting horses of the estate. Father and son walked through the castle grounds on foot. Trimmed hedges divided lawns far smoother than the coarse grass of the mountains, and a plethora of ornamental trees and bushes overhung a burn that meandered through the garden. A glance told Duncan that even the burn itself had been modified to create artificial waterfalls and rapids. This was an ordered world, constructed on the whim of a human mind. It bore no relation to the landscape in which he had grown up.

As they walked, surrounded by birdsong, Duncan was overcome by a creeping sense of unease.

White battlements rose above the trees ahead. A collection of square towers, some topped with spires and all dotted with tiny black windows, overlooked the gravel drive. It was a huge building, bigger by far than Duncan had expected, and he found himself staring at it as he walked.

Everything about the castle was big and bold and intended to convey the impression of both fabulous wealth and strength of arms, from the heraldic crest above the gatehouse to the Atholl Highlanders patrolling the grounds, dressed in tartan and armed with swords and rifles.

McAdie nudged his son with an elbow as they walked. 'Dinnae look the Duke in the eye, lad. Keep your head down and your mouth shut unless you are addressed directly. English only—he disnae speak Gaelic. Remember, he is your lord and master, and we live to serve him.'

'Aye, father.' Duncan wondered if he would be able to speak a word to the fearsome Duke even if he was required to. 'Tell me about him. What kind of man is he?'

His father merely grunted.

They scurried across the courtyard before the grand entrance hall which, like the rest of the castle, was built of massive stones cut square and topped with crenellations. A round tower on each side of the door made Duncan remember the stories his mother had told him as a child: tales of knights and towers, dragons and ghosts. He imagined archers watching from the shadowed galleries.

Of course, the front door was not for the likes of them. A footman let them into the servants' hall downstairs, a rat's maze of low ceilings and cold passageways. Duncan was astonished that even the servants lived in a building far larger than any he had seen in his life. They made their way to the kitchen, where the cook was butchering a deer carcass and shouting at his inferiors.

'Why in Christ's name is this knife not sharp? The next time you bring me a blunt knife I'll skewer you with it myself. Ah, McAdie! Are you looking for the butler? You there! Aye, you; go and fetch Mr Samson. Tell him McAdie and his son are here to see the master.'

The footman fled the room to find the butler. Duncan took the opportunity to examine his surroundings. He had often thought about whether a life of service might suit him better than a career outdoors. It paid well, they said, and there were opportunities for advancement; many butlers had started life as footmen. However, he had never actually seen the servants' hall of a great house before.

The kitchen was a dark and sooty chamber, dominated by a fireplace which had been fitted with a range: a black beast of iron that growled and rumbled, giving off vapours and noxious fumes. Pots and pans were everywhere—some neatly stacked, others dirty and piled by the sink—and the general atmosphere was one of frenzied chaos.

He watched the scullery maid as she bent over the sink washing dishes. For a moment she looked up, and their eyes met: her expression that of a startled fawn, eyes wide. She looked about fifteen years old.

Presently, the butler arrived and whisked them away from the kitchen. Mr Samson was a stooped fellow with a white face and even whiter hair: just a wisp of it rising from the top of his otherwise bald head, although his side-whiskers were profuse. His smile was immovable and somehow wistful, as if he looked down at the present day from the distant perspective of fifty years in the past, when the old master wore a powdered wig and carried a flintlock pistol at his belt to deter robbers.

'Is this your first visit to the castle, young man?'

His voice was exceedingly quiet, his tone gentle. Duncan had to strain to hear the words.

'Aye, sir.'

'I was younger than you when I first came here in the winter of 1780. The Mad Duke was just a bairn then.' He peered at Duncan more closely. 'You must be at least eighteen. Have you considered a career in service?'

'He most certainly has not,' McAdie interrupted. 'My boy's place is in the glen. I'll not see him become one of your lackeys, Samson.'

'I meant no offence,' the butler murmured in his amiable way. 'Life in the glens will get harder, of that you may be certain. Your son may require an alternative means of making his living ere too long.'

McAdie placed a warning hand on Samson's arm, and the two men faced each other in the hall: one tall and fierce, beard bristling, the other worn-out and frail. Samson's patient smile did not waver. McAdie must have realised this was not a fair contest for he released the butler after a moment.

'Is that a threat? Has the Duke said something?'

'It is merely an observation, Mr McAdie. The economy is changing day by day. No man's job is safe—not even yours.'

'It's a damned evil business,' McAdie muttered. 'Have I not served him well these thirty years?'

'Quite.' Samson's smile was a little cooler now, Duncan noticed. 'The master is waiting for you. I would advise you to remember your place when you speak to him.'

* * *

Duncan looked about himself in wonder. He had never seen so many books in one room before—and all shelved in the most opulent splendour. Why, even the chair in the corner was probably worth more than the McAdie family home.

The butler coughed discreetly. 'Alec McAdie and his son, your Grace.'

George Murray, the 6th Duke of Atholl, glanced up from his desk with a look of intense irritation. He was hunched over a ledger, writing in a rapid hand with a steel pen. He jabbed the nib in his ink pot and dashed off another line, then sighed and put the book to one side.

The Duke looked every bit as fearsome as Duncan had imagined. Although he was sitting down and therefore his height could not be judged, he had the stocky look of a fighting bull: more muscular in build than might be expected of a man who did not work with his hands. His imperious gaze, stern and without compassion, commanded authority. He had a curly brown beard and wore the regimental uniform of the Atholl Highlanders: dark coat, tartan cape, and white cross belt with silver buckle.

There was something strange in the way his eyes moved about the room. After a moment Duncan realised that the Duke was blind in his left eye.

'That will be all, Samson,' he said to the butler, who bowed and made his leave.

Now he stood and frowned at the visitors. McAdie kept his head respectfully bowed, but Duncan could not help staring—and for an instant their eyes met, master and lowliest estate worker. Duncan looked away, convinced he would be punished.

To his surprise, the Duke gave a hearty laugh and clapped Duncan on the back, almost sending him sprawling over the desk.

'Ha! Is this your boy, McAdie?'

'Aye, that he is, your Grace. Duncan is his name.'

'I like him. I like him a lot.' The Duke stroked his beard and poured himself a glass of whisky from the crystal decanter on his desk. 'Is he as tough as you?'

'He's young, but he has the mountains in his blood. He can chase a hart for twenty miles without tiring.'

'Good. I've thrown out old Hamish, so you will need strong and loyal men to assist you.'

McAdie's eyes widened. 'My lord? I thought Hamish was to retire in two years. He has work in him yet.'

'He's a damned insolent blackguard who has been conspiring with poachers to steal from me!' the Duke shouted, joviality gone in an instant. He slammed a fist down on his desk. The crystal rattled alarmingly. 'Villainy and disloyalty is rife among my servants. In these uncertain times I can no longer tolerate money draining away to no purpose. Did you know that the previous head housekeeper of Forest Lodge claimed ten pounds a year for candles? It's monstrous!'

McAdie shook his head, looking straight ahead at the wall. 'I had no idea.'

'Really? I wonder about that.' The Duke smiled, but Duncan thought it was the smile of a snake. 'Now that I am the Duke of Atholl in name at last, and not merely Lord Glenlyon running the estate in place of my mad uncle, I intend to trim the fat. There will be big changes in the Atholl glens. If you want your family to remain in my employment then you will have to prove your loyalty.'

Duncan remembered the confrontation between his father and the butler in the hall. Could it be true that the master was considering extending his deer forest and evicting the last remaining families in Glen Tilt? He would still need foresters, but the estate was full of ambitious young men, and Duncan's father was not as young or as strong as he once was.

He glanced at his father. McAdie was not the most emotionally expressive of men when it came to his deepest feelings, but Duncan could tell that he was in turmoil. If he felt resentment at being overlooked for the position of head keeper, he valued his status as *best* forester above all other things. Before entering the 5th Duke's service he had been a starving boy in rags, the survivor of a disastrous flood in Glen Garry which had obliterated his father's croft. Every ounce of pride he had was invested in his position as a senior forester of the Atholl estate.

'I will do anything you ask of me,' he whispered.

The Duke's temper had disappeared, and now he was businesslike again. 'Her Majesty the Queen and Prince Albert will be staying at Blair as my guests. You remember Prince Albert, don't you, McAdie? He remembers you most particularly. He's going stalking in my reserve and asked for you by name. He says you are the best.' The Duke stood very close to him now, staring into his eyes. 'It has not escaped my attention that you have served me for many years, and my guests consistently praise your abilities. Do you think you have the required talents to be head keeper here?'

'Aye, I do, m'lord. All I ask is the chance to prove it.'

'You will get that chance. Old Fraser will retire soon, and I'll need a replacement. The man who takes the job will need to be modern and ruthless in the application of his duties.'

The Duke turned to the window and looked out over the gardens, silent for some moments. When he turned, his expression had changed to a look of anxiety, perhaps even fear. Duncan wondered what the master of the estate could be afraid of.

'A lot depends on this visit,' the Duke went on. 'For the royal family to visit Blair twice in three years … well, it could transform my reputation. I want this estate to be renowned throughout Europe as the best place to hunt game and fish for salmon. Do you see that we shall all benefit if this goes well? Prince Albert is a great sportsman and he holds more power over all our lives than you could possibly realise.' The Duke spread his hands. 'If it should go badly, however, I shall be forced to take drastic measures to run my hold with greater economy. Do you understand me?'

Duncan understood perfectly. Naturally, the Duke wanted the best possible candidate for the next head keeper, and the coming hunt would be the perfect test of McAdie's loyalty and competence. If his father pleased Prince Albert and all went to plan then the family would keep their home and McAdie might even be considered for promotion. If his father failed, however—if the Prince was not pleased with his sport—then the Duke would find someone else to manage the estate, and all would come to ruin.

McAdie nodded. His expression conveyed resolve. 'Ye can trust me, your Grace. I'll not let you down.'

'Splendid,' the Duke said with a smile. 'Our guests arrive in two days. I know I can count on you both to make the necessary arrangements.'

QUEEN VICTORIA

CHAPTER II
VISITING ROYALTY

VICTORIA, QUEEN OF THE UNITED KINGDOM, was taking her young family to visit the Duke and Duchess of Atholl in their castle at Blair. The Queen looked out of her carriage window upon a landscape of romantic desolation and, to her eyes, unspeakable grandeur. The journey from Ardverikie that morning had taken them past lochs and forests, moors and ruins, mountain after mountain: a tableau of rugged natural charm, peopled by the hardy men and women who worked the land. Who would have thought that such wildness could exist in *her* kingdom, the jewel of modern civilisation?

I must remember that for my journal this evening, she thought.

As always, her attention was pulled in several directions at once. Little Bertie, dressed in his blue and white sailor suit, was fidgeting on the seat to her right and tugging his father's sleeve. Vicky, the Princess Royal, sat on Albert's lap and sang to herself.

A blur of movement caught Victoria's eye. Was that an eagle alighting from the treetop on the other side of the road—?

'Oh! Albert, look—it is an eagle.'

Her beloved husband turned his head to look, but the bird had already gone. He smiled at her, and in his expression, outwardly pensive yet tinged with a barely suppressed excitement, Victoria saw the man she had grown to adore. Others failed to see past the fact that he was a foreigner, or were fooled by his formal manners and stiff bearing. In private the real Albert shone through. He loved the outdoor life and in the wildness of Scotland he saw a little of the German countryside he had given up forever in order to be the husband of the British monarch.

The carriage turned a curve in the road, and green hills rolled into view, fringed with pinewoods and pastures where cattle grazed. *What a pity about the weather.* Dense cloud brushed the summit of the nearby hill, and a column of rain swept the sunlit lower flanks of a mountain a mile or so beyond. The contrasting colours delighted her and she wished she could preserve the image for future interpretation with her watercolours. Picture it: a rounded *beinn*, no higher than its neighbours but distinguished by nobler proportions and a lower slope of heather in full bloom, capped by pale rocks where nothing grew. This prow of stone, caught in a sunbeam, glowed white against a sky heavy with rain.

After a moment the sunbeam passed over and the vision faded.

Victoria loved the Highlands for this very reason. The interplay of landscape and sky enchanted every sense and remained constant for no more than a moment before some new change came upon the scene. She had fallen in love with the romance of this country.

'Do you see it, Albert?'

'Yes, *mein Lieb*,' Albert whispered in a voice meant only for her, reaching across the carriage to grip her hand. Their eyes met. The Prince of Wales was asleep and nodding his head, a happy smile on his young face.

* * *

Their welcome at Blair was, if possible, even grander than the reception at Ardverikie the previous day.

The gates of the estate stood open, and as the train of carriages passed through Victoria heard a shouted command from some hidden quarter. An instant later, the music of a hundred pipers and as many drummers burst like a storm over the silence of the village. Troops from the Duke's regiment lined the long avenue leading uphill into the estate, and opposite every tree a soldier dressed in tartan held his sword aloft and sang "God Save the Queen." The pipers marched in a column ahead of the royal carriage and Victoria found herself quite deafened by the cacophony.

Bertie awoke with a jolt and pressed his face to the glass, exclaiming "Bagpipes!" with delight as if he had never seen them before. The Princess Royal seemed less impressed and squirmed on her father's lap, scowling at the noise. Deer stood watching the procession in the meadows left of the avenue. Albert's gaze strayed in their direction for a moment before returning to his reverie, no doubt reflecting that little sport was to be had in shooting deer so domesticated. He had come here for wilder game.

They reached the castle. Footmen opened the carriage door and helped the royal couple to disembark, while the column of troops and pipers split in half and stood to attention on either side of the courtyard. A pennant on the highest tower fluttered in the breeze.

Lord and Lady Glenlyon—*no*, Victoria told herself, *I must not forget they are the Duke and Duchess of Atholl now*—stepped forward to greet them. The Duke was dressed in his formal military uniform as befitted the commander of the Atholl Highlanders, and Victoria thought his smile looked rather more relieved than genuine. After all, she had very nearly declined his invitation to visit Blair for a second time, careful to avoid the impression of favouritism.

The Duke bowed deeply. 'Welcome back to Blair, your Majesty. Once again I offer you the services of the Atholl Highlanders as your personal guard during the course of your stay, should you require it.'

Victoria smiled, most gratified by the splendid military display. She had presented the Atholl Highlanders with their colours two years ago.

'Thank you. We would like that very much.'

The Duke smiled. 'Then allow me to show you to your rooms. You must be fatigued after your journey.'

They began to climb the short flight of steps up to the front door. Behind them, Victoria's staff of servants and nannies began to unload their luggage and take care of the children.

'On the contrary,' Albert was saying, 'the beautiful countryside has provided a wonderful stimulant. I have been looking forward to returning to your estate ever since I heard the rumours about a champion stag. Are they true?'

The Duke's expression betrayed gratification for just a moment. Victoria did not miss it. She suspected the Duke had political or economic motives for inviting them back; not that she minded, for these people had been good to the royal household over the years.

'We shall discuss the matter after dinner if it is agreeable to you,' the Duke said with only the slightest hint of triumph in his voice.

* * *

Forbes coughed into his handkerchief, leaving a stain of blood.

He stared at it for a moment before folding the square of cloth and secreting it in a pocket. The innkeeper was staring at him over the bar, which consisted of little more than a plank of wood over the top of two barrels.

'Are ye well, m'lord?'

Forbes coughed again. 'I am not your lord, merely a traveller.'

The innkeeper—Todd of Todd's Inn, Pitlochry—looked nervous. He was a shortish man, full in both beard and belly.

'D'ye need a room?'

Forbes dumped his knapsack on the bare floorboards. 'No, no; merely a recommendation. I am in need of a guide to the Cairngorms. He must be strong, knowledgeable, and utterly trustworthy.' He smiled. 'I am a stranger to these parts and would appreciate any help you can give me.'

Todd remained stiff in manner and did not respond to his friendly words. 'Are ye with the Queen's retinue? One o' Prince Albert's shooting companions, maybe?'

'No! I am a scientist, if you must know, and wish to travel through the Atholl glens.'

The innkeeper shook his head emphatically. 'No man in this town will take you through his Lordship's reserve. He is harsh with trespassers.'

Forbes cursed the obstinacy of his countrymen. In Switzerland, the uplands belonged to nobody, the innkeepers were an obliging breed who would go to any lengths to satisfy their guests, and guides were noble creatures of the most superior qualities. Was it too much to ask the same of his own kinsmen?

'What would you have me do?'

'Go back to Edinburgh. There's nought but heather and peat hags out there—certainly no object that might interest a learned man such as yourself, sir, if you'll excuse the impertinence.'

Forbes sighed. He would get no help here.

* * *

Duncan had memorised his father's instructions before leaving. *Take the pony to Pitlochry to be shod, collect the post if there is any, and buy provisions. Meet me at the Falls of Tarf in three days.*

Pitlochry wasn't much of a place to look at; certainly not as large or as grand as the cities he had heard about, but it was the largest settlement in the area and, to his eyes, a veritable metropolis. It had grown rapidly in recent years. These days rich folk from the towns came here for the healthful mountain air, which Duncan found ironic since so many of the local Highlanders were desperate to escape their failing agricultural way of life and start anew in the towns. Pitlochry now boasted two modest coaching inns, a post office, a bank, and a general store.

He took every opportunity to visit Pitlochry. It was a change of scenery from the windswept moors, and besides, one day maybe he would be a rich townsman with his own business and a bank account. Who knew when the first opportunity for advancement would appear?

After completing his chores, Duncan left Floraidh grazing by the river and made for Todd's Inn. He only had a few coins left in his pocket but it would be enough to buy a draught of ale. His father would not approve, of course—alcohol was for consumption on the hill and nowhere else according to the old forester—but Duncan felt conscious of how awkward and out of place he must look amongst the worldly-wise townsfolk. He wanted to fit in.

The door to the inn opened as he approached, and a gentleman stepped out, holding the door for him.

Something in the dispirited expression on the man's face made Duncan take a second glance. The fact that he did not wear Highland dress marked him as a stranger immediately. He was dressed in a black coat and white neckcloth, carried a staff, and wore stout hobnailed boots. He was a tall man and yet somehow diminished in stature, stooped and thin, suggestive of someone who had once been uncommonly strong but had lost his active build due to some lingering illness.

Their eyes met. Duncan's first thought was that the stranger had the face of a poet: large and expressive eyes, sad somehow, and a small mouth. His skin was very pale and looked delicate, like waxed paper.

'*Feasgar math,*' Duncan said, wishing him a good evening in the native language of the Highlands.

The stranger paused at the threshold. 'I'm sorry? I'm afraid I don't speak Gaelic.'

'Good evening,' he repeated in English.

'And to you, my boy.'

That would have been the end of the conversation, were it not for a detail that caught Duncan's eye. Protruding from the top of the man's knapsack was a complex scientific instrument, a device of brass and hinges, varnished wood and scuffed leather. Inspiration seized Duncan. This gentleman, he felt certain, was a man of wealth and importance. Why else would he have brought such an item to a place like this?

The young Highlander sensed an opportunity.

He laid a hand on the man's arm as he walked past. 'Just a moment, sir. Will ye let me buy you a drink?'

* * *

'I am in need of a guide to the Mounth and the Cairngorms. Are you familiar with those hills?'

Duncan took a gulp of his ale, feeling pleased with himself. He had caught himself a Professor—from Edinburgh, no less—and one who would pay good money for a guide through the mountains! The investment of two

PROFESSOR FORBES

pence for the ale would turn out to be a profitable one, of that he felt sure. Who could tell where this opportunity might lead?

'I am your man,' Duncan said confidently. 'I was born in Glen Tilt and know the reserve better than anyone.'

Duncan was conscious that the stranger was studying him. Once again he was struck by the uncommonly intelligent look in those eyes: shrewd, calculating, the expression of a man who worked with his head rather than his hands.

'Can you use a theodolite or clinometer? Can you perform mental arithmetic?'

Duncan shook his head. He did not know what those words meant.

'Have you any education at all?'

'I can read the Bible.'

Forbes closed his eyes and sighed. 'I suppose that will have to do. Now, what is it I hear about the Duke of Atholl persecuting travellers on his land? I cannot do my work if I am to be interfered with.'

'Ach, you dinnae want to be paying too much attention to that, sir,' Duncan said hurriedly, anxious not to frighten away his first real job. 'Besides, I work for the Duke.'

'And the Bodach?' Forbes said with a smile.

Despite his confidence, Duncan shivered.

'There are … certain places where travellers are not safe. Ye'd do well to listen to the auld tales, Professor. They hold many truths.'

Forbes still wore his knowing smile. 'All right. Now to discuss payment. I offer two pounds if you can guide me through Glen Tilt.'

Two pounds! That was more than his father earned in a month.

Although tempted, Duncan considered his situation. He had to be at the Falls of Tarf at the north border of the estate in less than three days. A great deal depended on the outcome of the royal hunt, and if he missed the rendezvous then his father would punish him severely. However, why should he not take on a little extra work? It would hurt nobody. This Professor looked harmless enough, and Duncan knew how to keep out of sight in the glens. He would take the Professor to where he needed to go and then join his father and Prince Albert on the stalk.

He had a few doubts, but ignored them. This could be the start of the better life he had dreamed about.

'Aye, I'll do it,' he said finally. They shook hands, and the bargain was made.

* * *

Forbes had begun to suspect that the pony didn't like him. In appearance it was a perfectly ordinary Highland pony: short and powerful, covered in a pelt of mottled brown hair that extended from its mane to the very hooves that clawed for purchase in the dust of the road. Before leaving Pitlochry Duncan had laden the animal with a huge variety of provisions: food and cloth to make clothing, blankets, guns, powder and lead to make rifle balls, and a case of tea. The goods were wrapped in oilskins and stowed in baskets slung from each side of the pony. Forbes suspected the creature must be unevenly laden, for it seemed to be continually veering to one side and trying to force him off the side of the track.

The first part of their journey took them through a wooded gorge that reminded him of the Alps. Steep hillsides grew thick with birch and beech, rowan and stunted oak, every branch bearded with moss. Occasionally they passed clearings which offered glimpses down into the ravine beneath: a stone-choked slot where the waters of the Tilt boiled over slabs of rock and thundered over drops.

As a geologist, Forbes respected this place. In 1785, James Hutton had discovered granite penetrating the older metamorphic schists in the bed of the river: a discovery that led him to theorise that the world was incalculably ancient, and that the land was not a static thing but a constantly evolving geological process.

This was the place where the science of geology had won its first battle against superstition and ignorance. He thought it fitting that this would be the place where he would consolidate his own career as a field geologist.

Although Duncan had been talkative enough at the inn, he did not speak much as they walked. The evening was quiet and humid, and the dreaded Highland midges were out in force. Millions of the bloodsuckers haunted the riverbank, clinging to the undersides of ferns and the purple blooms of heather. When awoken from their dormant state they billowed up in vast, silent clouds, engulfing the party and landing on every exposed inch of flesh, biting with their vicious little jaws. The pony plodded on without complaint, merely swatting at the insects with her tail, but Forbes was driven to distraction by the constant attacks.

Remarkably, Duncan seemed oblivious.

'How do you cope with these infernal beasts?' Forbes cried after half an hour of torment. 'How does anyone get any work done in the mountains at this time of year?'

'Folk generally get used to them.'

The onslaught diminished as the light faded and the temperature dropped. The sunset painted flecks of red and gold on the delicate tracery of cloud to the west, portentous of bad weather at some point in the future, Forbes thought, although in the present it made an exceedingly picturesque scene. Looking ahead, hills rose to dominate the skyline: a rolling landscape of wind and heather, water and snow, granite tor and shattered corrie.

He concentrated on the physical act of walking for a while. Small stones crunched under the hobnailed soles of his boots, which were fortunately well broken-in and would be unlikely to rub or blister his feet. So far, praise God, his health had caused no impediment to the journey. Now that he had some purpose to occupy his thoughts and moderate exercise for his limbs, he found the pain in his abdomen no longer caused such worry or distraction.

The point of his alpenstock clattered against a stone. He realised that it had grown dark very quickly, and upon checking his watch discovered that the time was gone nine o'clock.

'Have you brought a lantern?' Forbes asked his guide.

Duncan stopped and waited for Forbes to catch up. He cut a slight figure in the twilight, shrewd eyes constantly scanning the wooded hillsides on either side of the river. Forbes was surprised by the wiry strength of the lad. He couldn't be much older than eighteen, and yet already he was as muscular and sinewy, in his compact way, as a man ten years his senior. His Highland dress was evocative of a traditional way of life. In Edinburgh nobody wore the kilt. Duncan's kilt was a simple garment of the Atholl tartan, repaired in one or two places, although its quality set it above the poor homespun cloth often worn by crofters. He wore long woollen socks and laced brogues which didn't appear to be nailed. The only sign of the nineteenth century in his attire was the waistcoat and grey cloth jacket which had probably come from a tailor in one of the nearby towns.

'No lantern,' Duncan replied. 'We'll be at my house in a few hours.'

'As you wish,' Forbes said, but he could not help feeling a little anxious. Why had Duncan insisted they set out so late in the evening, and without a lamp? It would have been more logical to take lodgings in Pitlochry overnight and begin the journey early in the morning.

'It widnae do to be caught out by the bad weather on the way,' Duncan explained, anticipating Forbes' next question.

* * *

Alec McAdie stood with the eighteen other servants of Blair Castle around the long table in the servants' hall. Delicious smells emanated from the dishes Angus had placed before them, filled to the brim with game pie and potato stew. The butler took his place at the head of the table and cast a sombre glance over his little kingdom.

'For what we are about to receive may we be truly thankful,' he intoned. One of the footmen made a move to sit down, but Samson stopped him with a sharp look. 'One moment. I believe that on this auspicious occasion a prayer is in order. Lord, may you guide and protect Her Majesty, Queen Victoria, and help her find favour in this house and all who reside within it. We ask this not for ourselves but so that we may continue to do Your work. Amen.'

'Amen,' McAdie said with the others, although his cynical nature led him to believe that Samson's prayer was more selfish than he was willing to admit. Nobody in this household wanted to lose their position.

They sat down and tucked in to the food on offer. McAdie helped himself to a generous portion of the pie and as many potatoes as he could fit on his plate. He had no qualms about eating well: his status as a senior forester, and the contribution he made to this estate, entitled him to a little extra reward. Besides, the food at home was both basic and monotonous. His diet usually consisted of oatcakes and porridge.

When I am head keeper I shall eat pie and potatoes every month, he mused.

'Where did you get these potatoes, Angus?' he asked of the cook, who was attacking his food with vigour at the other end of the table. 'I cannae recall the last time I ate a potato.'

'A trader from Blairgowrie,' he replied in between mouthfuls. 'The blight has not been so severe there.'

McAdie felt thankful that he was able to partake in such a feast when thousands of his countrymen were starving, many of them emigrating to America in search of a better life. The potato blight had crippled Scotland. He thanked God that, as a servant of the Atholl estate, he and his family were insulated from such troubles ... unless, of course, the Duke should decide to terminate his employment.

A chill ran through his body. McAdie knew what it was like to be without a home, without a position, without anything but the rags in which he lived and slept every day. He would do anything to save his family from that fate.

A bell rang somewhere in the hall. Samson looked up, then smiled at one of the footmen.

'That's the drawing room bell. Go and see what the master wants, boy.'

McAdie continued to eat. The footman returned in minutes, panting with exertion from running up and down several flights of stairs.

'Mr McAdie is wanted upstairs in the red drawing room. Prince Albert has asked to see him.'

Every face turned to look at McAdie. He put down his knife and fork, wiped his mouth with a napkin, and stood to leave the table. He clasped his hands behind his back to hide the fact that they were trembling.

Accompanied by the butler, he made the journey upstairs to the drawing room. As ever he was stunned by the grandeur of the castle. When he was surrounded by such fabulous wealth, why would the Duke ever need to take drastic action to raise more cash? It made no sense to him, but then again he was a simple man who did not understand the ways of the nobility. Some gentlemen, it was said, lost thousands of pounds betting on horses, or invested their fortunes in railway companies that failed to make any money. In such uncertain times even the rich were not entirely insulated from the troubles of the wider world.

Mr Samson pushed open the white doors to the drawing room, announced the name of the visitor, and swiftly departed.

If McAdie had thought the rest of the house opulent, the drawing room dazzled him. Red wallpaper led the eye up to a finely carved ceiling. The fireplace was framed by classical white pillars and more delicate scroll-work. Paintings of Highland scenes, and portraits of aristocratic ancestors, hung from the walls. Even the carpet represented greater wealth than the entire population of Glen Tilt could show for its labours. Tall windows along one side of the room flooded the space with light, and although McAdie considered himself a simple fellow he instinctively felt that this room was designed to show off the Duke's wealth and power.

The master of the house stood by the fireplace, hand on the hilt of his sword. His wife, the Duchess, was poised on a chair at his side, hands clasped at her lap. She wore the sort of enormous flowing dress McAdie had often seen the womenfolk of the gentry dressed up in: spectacular but impractical. Her expression was hard and canny as a fox.

Prince Albert sat opposite the master and mistress of the house. He was a tall man, and carried himself with a stiff, formal bearing. With a balding pate and rather ordinary mutton-chop whiskers and moustache, McAdie had always thought Albert looked more like a banker's clerk than the consort of the Queen. He wore regular country attire: tartan breeches, waistcoat, neckcloth, and a grey morning coat. There was certainly no sign of a crown or any overt indications of wealth. Although McAdie had found the Prince an amiable enough man in conversation, it would not do to forget that he was King in all but name.

'Victoria is with the children presently,' Albert was saying in his mild way to the Duchess. 'They are tired after the journey and wished to rest.'

McAdie stood by the door, waiting to be acknowledged. After a few seconds the Duke looked at him.

'Come here, McAdie.'

He walked towards the comfortable chairs in the centre of the room, acutely aware of his rough mountain clothes and dirty shoes.

Prince Albert smiled at him. 'Ah, my favourite … what is the word? Gill-ly?'

'The word is ghillie, your Highness,' McAdie ventured. 'Although I'm a senior forester. Ghillie is a junior term.'

'The man who makes the deer come when I wish to shoot them,' the Prince said with a chuckle. 'I admire the hill folk of your country: strong, wise, loyal, and knowledgeable, quite unlike the surly agitators we have in Bavaria. In Scotland the proper order of things is respected. I love this beautiful and wild country more with every visit.'

The Duke and Duchess laughed politely at that remark, but McAdie kept his expression neutral. For some reason Prince Albert had taken a liking to him on his previous visit.

McAdie had been forced to make conversation and respond to questions from the Prince for days. He was as deferential to his betters as the next man—often more so—but even he was sensible of the injustice at the heart of society, and thanked God daily for his good fortune in having a position in service of a great estate. If he were ever forced to join the ranks of the starving multitudes once again, he too may be tempted to take up arms against the rulers and demand fair pay, universal employment, and lower food prices.

As things stood, he would smile and do the bidding of his masters, and if his pride was sometimes a little wounded by their remarks, he would consider it a small price to pay for having a roof over his head and food on the table when so many had neither.

'So, McAdie,' Albert continued. 'Murray tells me of a hart with fourteen tines on his antlers. A ... *kaiserlichen Hirsch*?'

'An imperial stag,' the Duke translated. 'He is the greatest beast of my estate, although in August he often ventures north, into the forest of Mar. They call him Damh-mor.'

McAdie noticed a look of satisfaction passing between the Duke and his wife, and the forester wondered if this conversation had been engineered specifically to get Albert interested in the champion stag. After all, such a tale, told by the Prince back in London, might work wonders in increasing the prestige of the Atholl estate.

Albert leaned forward, visibly intrigued. 'Is it possible to stalk this creature? McAdie, what is your opinion?'

The forester blinked in surprise. He had not expected to be involved in this conversation as an equal. 'He's a mere beast like any other, sir.' He saw the Duke's warning look, and decided to improvise. '...which isnae to say he'll be an easy target. He's a cunning creature who has escaped many a time. They say he's roamed the Mounth for hundreds o' years.'

Prince Albert clapped his hands together, eyes sparkling. 'He will be mine. You will find him for me, McAdie.'

'Aye, sir.'

'I have promised the Queen I shall be away from the castle for no longer than a day.' He looked a trifle embarrassed at stating his wife's condition, but his tone was earnest. 'Can it be done?'

McAdie cleared his throat. Most hunts lasted less than twenty four hours, but it was by no means unusual to chase a hart for two or three days if their target was a particularly cunning one—and none was more cunning than Damhmor. The estate was vast, and the Mar estate to the north larger still.

He felt uneasy swearing to Prince Albert that he could find and corner the hart within a day, but then he saw the Duke's piercing glare and knew he could not refuse.

'Aye, I'll do it, sir; rest easy on that account.'

Albert smiled and returned to small talk with his hosts. So now McAdie knew precisely what was required of him: a successful stalk in which the strongest and most cunning hart of the estate would fall to Prince Albert. Could he pass the test? He had the skills, of that he was certain; but luck plays a big part in any stalk, and much could go wrong.

* * *

Forbes was exhausted by the time they reached Lochain Lodge. As young Duncan had predicted, cloud had come in from the east and obscured the moonlight, leaving him to stumble along in darkness. To make matters worse, the road had turned to a mere path long ago: a fragmented ribbon of stones and mud, weaving its way between spurs of land, intersected by burns, often disappearing into a morass of swampy ground that only the pony seemed to be able to cross without becoming overwhelmed in the quagmire. He clutched his staff and tapped the ground just ahead of him like a blind man. Robbed of his sense of sight and the greater landscape to occupy his thoughts, the pain returned, and with it the creeping fear of what the future might hold for him.

'We're here, Professor,' Duncan said at last. 'This is my home. We can stop for a few hours of rest.'

Forbes leaned against his staff. 'A few hours?'

'Aye, until dawn—then we must be away.'

Why did they have to leave at dawn? Why not stop for a proper rest? Forbes was reluctant to share his infirmities with his guide, but perhaps he could claim tiredness.

'I confess...' he began, then gasped as a spasm of pain ripped through his side. 'I am fatigued by the journey. I am not used to walking at such a pace for so long.'

Duncan remained silent. Forbes could not make out his expression in the darkness.

'I fail to see why you are in such a hurry. Can we not stay until a decent hour of the morning?' Forbes pleaded.

'No,' Duncan said shortly.

The boy opened a door. Light streamed out, dazzling Forbes and causing him to stumble. When his vision had recovered, he saw that the doorway led to the interior of a mountain cottage, constructed of rough-hewn granite blocks and no larger than a barn. A blast of warm air, smelling agreeably of peat smoke, greeted the travellers.

Duncan unloaded the baskets of goods from the pony and carried them through the doorway, thumping and scraping against the stones embedded in the earth floor.

'*Halò màthair…*' Forbes heard him say.

'*Duncan! Fàilte dhachaidh!*'

Forbes could not translate the Gaelic phrases, but the sentiment of welcome was obvious enough. He leaned his staff against the outside wall and stepped into the warm haven of Lochain Lodge.

The first thing he noticed was that the building consisted of a single room, rectangular in plan, with the fireplace to the left and the sleeping area to the right. A curtain of homespun cloth partially hid the beds, which appeared to be wooden pallets laid directly on the floor and spread with blankets and sheepskins. No carpet was in evidence; in fact, furnishings of any kind were few in number and old in appearance. The megalithic table was deeply scarred from decades of use. Three stools crowded around the table and a cupboard with carved doors was mounted on the wall left of the fireplace; on the other side, beneath a row of shelves straining under the weight of stone jars, was a simple piece of framed embroidery depicting a Gaelic verse. Items of all description hung from the rafters: clothing, ropes, baskets, guns, oilskins, sacks of oatmeal, racks of smoked fishes, a side of venison. A single oil lamp lit the room.

A middle-aged woman had risen from her stool and was conversing with Duncan in the rapid, musical tongue of the Highlands. She glanced at the visitor and folded her arms, foot tapping nervously on the floorboards. Forbes thought she looked like a heron, thin and bony, attention flitting nervously from here to there as she tried to assess whether the newcomer was a friend or an enemy.

'He only speaks English,' Duncan said after a moment, turning to look at Forbes. 'He is a Professor all the way from Edinburgh.'

'What if your father finds out? He could be a poacher!'

Duncan laughed out loud. 'Look at him, *màthair*. He disnae even have a rifle.'

'Then why is he here?'

Forbes stepped forward. 'If I might be permitted to explain,' he said gently, taking the woman's hands in his own. 'I am, as your son has revealed, a Professor at the University of Edinburgh. My subject of expertise is geology.'

The woman's expression remained mistrustful. She had been an uncommonly handsome woman once, Forbes realised. Streaks of gold still remained in her hair, which was largely grey now and bound up in a bun, tied in place with a short length of ribbon.

'I study rocks, mountains, rivers, and glaciers,' he elaborated. 'That is why I'm here.'

Her expression told him she did not understand. He'd found that people who lived among mountains often had little curiosity about them: with a few exceptions, they regarded mountains as sources of income or as nuisances, and if they thought about them at all it was for purely practical reasons.

'To study our mountains? Why?'

Good question.

'Because nobody except me ever has. If I'm not welcome then I will find shelter elsewhere, but I would be greatly honoured if you would accept me as your guest. I have heard good things about Highland hospitality!'

She pulled her hands away and blushed like a young girl. After a moment her tension seemed to evaporate, and she even went so far as to permit a shy smile. Forbes wondered how long it was since she had last had a guest to entertain.

'Ach well, perhaps you're harmless after all. You'll have to be gone afore Mr McAdie gets home, though.'

* * *

Duncan watched the visitor eat and drink. Mother had offered him the best victuals, of course: cuts of smoked venison, oatcakes, and a bowl of Atholl Brose. The Professor seemed to be enjoying his feast. Duncan, by contrast, ate only an oatcake and washed it down with a draught of water from the burn. He had picked up the habit of eating little from his father. Foresters could not move fast and silently on a full stomach.

His mother's reaction had brought into sharp focus the punishment that would await him if his father found out what he had done. To invite a stranger into the Duke's reserve, at a time when poaching was rife, was surely a terrible crime; and yet, could Duncan really be blamed for making the most of an opportunity? Besides, he told himself, Forbes was harmless and he would be long gone before Albert's retinue reached the borders of the estate at the Falls of Tarf.

Timing and confidence were everything. Fortunately these were skills he had learned out on the stalk.

The Professor lay down and went to sleep immediately after his supper, and Duncan helped his mother clear away the food. 'I ken what I'm doing,' he whispered to her. 'Dinnae fash yerself.'

She looked up with a worried expression, caught as ever between the desire to provide a better life for her son, and the deeply ingrained sense of loyalty to her husband. Sadly the two desires were often in conflict and it grieved Duncan to see how much pain this caused his mother. *If I can take you away from this place when I leave, I will do it,* he thought.

'I hope so, *beagan*. When will your father leave Blair?'

'Dawn. Happen they'll breakfast at Forest Lodge as usual.' He smiled with pride. 'Father was personally asked to attend to Prince Albert. There was talk of promotion!'

His mother gave a little gasp of pleasure and covered her mouth with a hand. 'At last!' An anxious look gradually stole over her features again, and the worry lines around her eyes grew more prominent in the light of the oil lamp. 'Your father told me about the last time Albert came to visit. He asked about the oldest hart of the estate. What if they go after Damh-mor?'

Duncan thought about that for a moment. Of course, it made perfect sense: Prince Albert was a famed sportsman, and as visiting royalty he would naturally want to bag the greatest prize.

'It will be awful bad luck if they shoot him,' his mother continued. 'That beast is hundreds of years old, *beagan*...'

'Now then, *màthair*,' he said, covering her hand with his own for a moment and smiling fondly. 'That isnae true. He's a stag just like all the others.'

'He belongs to the Bodach of Mar,' she whispered, expression still fearful. 'I hope they dinnae catch him.'

Duncan did not reply. Years of work out amongst the master's herds had taught him that deer were just deer and nothing more, and yet every estate had legends of a beast older and wiser than all the others. Disaster and misfortune would befall anyone who dared slay such creatures.

Would the prize be worth the cost?

* * *

The weather broke at dawn.

Alec McAdie was angry with himself for not recognising the signs. Had he been too wrapped up in his own concerns to notice the weather approaching from the east? Wind howled down from the heights of Carn Liath, blowing spray from the River Tilt and sending up an ominous groan and murmur from the pinewoods of the lower estate. The herd of tame deer that grazed the castle gardens was nowhere to be seen. Ravens wheeled overhead, fighting the gusts, keen eyes watching for small creatures crushed by falling branches.

The first spots of rain began to fly as Prince Albert stepped out from the castle's doorway. McAdie waited in the courtyard with one of the other foresters, Thomas, who was smoking a clay pipe and squinting into the heavens with a bloodshot eye, muttering darkly about portents.

'It's going to be a muckle storm and nae mistake, McAdie...'

'Ach, we've had worse in the auld Duke's day, and brought home a dozen harts for the table. Have you brought the whisky?'

Thomas tapped first one side of his jacket, which rang like a bell, and then the other, which did likewise. 'Two bottles, aye, and plenty more in the saddlebags. I'll take nae chances when the weather's like this.'

'Good man.'

Albert was dressed in ordinary shooting gear: thick tweed jacket, cap, and rather garish tartan trousers. He stood under the cornice above the door and peered into the sky, absent-mindedly stroking his moustache as he did so.

He looked back into the open door. '*Das Wetter ist schlecht, Isaac.*'

A servant emerged, heavily laden with baggage and guns. He was dressed in a manner that made McAdie fight to suppress a laugh: short trousers held up by braces, long red socks, and an absurd little peaked cap with a feather in it. Could that costume really be what German hunters wore when stalking their prey? McAdie wondered if the stags would die laughing at the first sight of them.

Thomas raised an eyebrow. 'Wha' the—?'

'Wheesht! Do ye want to be horse-whipped by the Duke?'

The German servant, Isaac, exchanged a few words with Albert before struggling over to the far side of the courtyard and depositing his load in the cart. He turned to look at the Highlanders who watched him silently. Isaac had the polished and refined look of a member of the gentry, and yet he was a servant, no more of a gentleman than McAdie was. He had curly black hair and a neat little moustache, but no side-whiskers to speak of. A mocking little smile crossed his lips for a moment before he looked away and returned to attend his master.

'How come he gets tae use the front door?' Thomas muttered.

The bearded figure of the Duke emerged from the castle, magnificently attired in kilt and tweed jacket, *sgian-dubh* sheathed at his side. He strode out into the yard and beamed as the rain fell on his face. McAdie was glad to see his master in good humour.

'Morning all!' the Duke boomed. 'We shall have good honest Scottish weather for our outing. Any stragglers? McAdie there! Have you brought provisions suitable for our royal guest?'

McAdie bowed. 'My son is bringing the victuals. He's meeting us at the northern border of the estate.'

The Duke rubbed his hands together as he paced to and fro, examining the items being loaded into the cart and patting the pony on the head. 'He had better be there, then! No dogs today?'

'Damh-mor is wary of hounds. We'll have more luck without them.'

He turned back towards Albert. 'Do you have everything you require, my friend?'

The Prince stepped out into the rain and smiled as a gust blew a volley of droplets into his face. To his credit, he did not shrink away from the weather as McAdie had seen many a time from visiting nobles. That was a good sign. Perhaps he would be a steady man on the hill after all. The Duke's boisterous good humour seemed to be raising the spirits of the entire party.

'Perhaps a … how do you say it? Um-brella?'

The Duke laughed again. 'Alas, it would frighten the harts. Now, will you introduce Isaac to my men?'

The German Jaeger stood beside and slightly behind the Prince. At his master's command he stepped forward to shake hands with the foresters. McAdie did not like him. His gaze was altogether too superior, his smile too false; he had, in short, the air of a man who believed himself to be of better stock than the other servants. No doubt that was why he had not made his presence known in the servants' hall. Why, even Albert's German valets had come downstairs to exchange a friendly word with their Scottish counterparts, and Victoria's staff mingled freely with the other servants.

The Duke's manner became serious as he drew the party around him. 'A small matter before we begin. Dangerous men patrol these glens: ruffians, poachers, criminals of the most base kind who have made a nuisance of themselves recently. I have spoken to Isaac here, and he will be on his guard against any attacks. If anything happens, we shall break off the hunt and return to Blair. Albert's safety is of prime importance.'

'Nonsense,' Albert protested, but Isaac was nodding at the Duke's warning. McAdie thought the Jaeger's expression conveyed a certain degree of relish at the prospect of being attacked by footpads.

'Another thing,' the Duke continued. 'In this castle you and I may be the masters, Albert, but out there on the moor we must all defer to McAdie here. Our chase may take us deep into the forest of Mar, land McAdie knows better than any other man in my service. If we want to catch Damhmor we will have to carry out his orders.'

McAdie did not dare meet the Duke's gaze. He was well aware that he was being tested, and that the Duke did not in reality hold his abilities in such esteem; nevertheless, he would do his duty and bring back the champion hart, God willing. This was the test of his life. If he failed he would never be able to forgive himself for losing his last chance for advancement. Worse, he would never be able to look his son in the eye again.

Albert bowed to the forester and reached out to take his hand. McAdie trembled a little as he shook hands with the Prince, and, encouraged by the gesture, he looked up and met his gaze. McAdie did not believe himself to a be a particularly good judge of character—he understood animals better than men—but in that face, a little plumper than the Albert depicted by the famous engravings of his marriage to the Queen, McAdie thought he saw a certain integrity and honesty. *I think I can trust this man,* he allowed, although his underlying cynicism always prescribed caution.

'Lead and I will follow,' Albert said to him.

CHAPTER III
THE BATTLE OF TARF WATER

FORBES WAS DETERMINED NOT TO SHOW any sign of weakness to his guide, but this pace was killing him.

'Please, Duncan; a little slower.'

Duncan stopped and looked back, that impatient look in his eyes again. The pony turned to one side of the path and started munching on a tussock of grass. It took a long time for Forbes to catch up with them. The path seemed fearfully steep, the ground uneven and boggy beneath the soles of his boots, and the pain in his gut punched him with every step.

Rain sluiced down from the heavens, painting the landscape a miserable brown. His clothing had long since soaked through to the skin. Only the energy generated by his uphill struggle kept him warm, but the constant battle against the wind, which was trying very hard to bowl him off the path and into the burn on the other side, drained his reserves. Tattered rags of mist blasted past on both sides. If there were mountains anywhere nearby, the weather obscured them from view.

Forbes began to wonder if he had been foolish in accepting the challenge of Bràigh Riabhach after all. They had been travelling for many hours—had left Blair and Pitlochry far, far behind—and yet the great peaks of the Cairngorms were still miles to the north. Could he make it there without killing himself? Even if he could make the journey, would he be in any fit condition to do his work and return home? For a man who had once taken pride in his ability to climb the hardest peaks, to do the work of science in the harshest of places, this was a low moment in his career.

I am a shadow of the man I was five years ago. This is pitiful.

'We cannae slow down, Professor. We must keep moving, else...'

He didn't finish his sentence. Not for the first time, Forbes wondered why this young man was in such a hurry. A working man would have other commitments, of course, but Forbes didn't like the shifty look in his eye sometimes. He was certain Duncan had not told him everything.

Forbes drew level with the pony and stopped for a moment, leaning against his staff and breathing hard. 'Else what, my boy? Are you afraid of meeting one of the other gamekeepers, perhaps ... one who would take a dim view of this intrusion into the Duke's reserve? If there is something you have to tell me then I had better hear it at once.'

Being stern did not come naturally to him, but sometimes the firm approach worked with native guides. In Switzerland, he had found the peasants of Val d'Herens easy to control if given clear orders. By contrast, Chamouniards were more independent and were likely to abandon their master in some lonely place if spoken to in such a manner. In Scotland there were no professional mountain guides.

Duncan folded his arms and turned to look Forbes square in the eyes. His face, although youthful, had an angular hardness to it that reflected the landscape in which he had grown up. He seemed not to even notice the wind and rain.

Forbes realised at once that the stern approach would not work with him.

'Ye wanted me to take ye to the northern border of the estate, aye?'

'Those were the original terms of your engagement, yes.'

'We're nearly there. After that I'll be on my way. I've got work to do, ken?'

Duncan turned and resumed his march at the same efficient pace as before. The pony flashed Forbes a filthy look—he was convinced the animal hated him—and flicked her tail to disperse a cloud of midges.

Forbes cursed his lack of foresight. He was used to the Alps, where guides made their living from guiding alone and thrived on cultivating long-lasting relationships with their clients. Dear Auguste Balmat would think nothing of being asked to extend an engagement for another week. Why had he not thought to engage Duncan on an open-ended contract?

The fact is, he needed his guide. He could not afford to lose Duncan at the Falls of Tarf.

'Wait,' he called out. 'I will pay you double if you agree to accompany me into the Forest of Mar.'

'I cannae do that, sir,' Duncan said without turning or breaking his stride. 'I am needed by the Duke, and that's the end of it.'

* * *

Alec McAdie pressed his body to the ground. Water seeped through his clothing from the rich carpet of moss beneath, but he hardly noticed; the discomforts of the job were oddly satisfying, and he was proud of the fact that he could endure any weather, no matter how inclement, without a word. Besides, a generous slug of *uisge-beatha* ten minutes ago had fortified his body against the cold.

Careful to avoid any sudden movement, he reached up to tease a branch of heather out of the way, then slid his telescope through the gap. The telescope was his most prized possession. It had been given to him by a former head keeper of the estate, John Crerar, when he retired. Crerar claimed the telescope had once been carried by a sea captain at the Battle of the Nile, but McAdie doubted that claim; nevertheless, it was a good glass which had served him well.

He looked through the eyepiece and made a tiny adjustment to the focus. The landscape sprang into view.

Despite poor visibility, he recognised every feature on the hillside ahead. There, at the bottom of the slope, the torrent of Allt Mheann leapt between boggy pools on its way down from An Sligearnach. A windswept plateau of purple heather, pock-marked by peat hags and the occasional rock, overlooked the gorge where the Tarf water emptied itself into the young River Tilt. Burns foamed down channels in the hills which had been dry this time the day before. The mountains were shedding their burden of rain.

He saw movement down there in the glen. The rain and mist obscured his view of the ford where Duncan would be waiting with supplies; however, the movement was even more distant, some way along the gorge leading into the Mar forest. They were very near the border between the two estates now.

McAdie shifted his telescope, and that was when he saw the deer.

A few beasts were grazing near the flat *bealach* about a mile away: seven younger stags, maybe two or three years old, and four older animals. At this range he could not see any details, but one of the stags was a big one. Could it be Damh-mor? This was his usual August stomping ground, although he had heard from the Mar foresters that he sometimes went up into the distant corries of Cairn Toul and Bràigh Riabhach. The legend of the Bodach overshadowed those lonely places and no forester would follow a hart there under normal circumstances.

McAdie sniffed the air. The wind was still in the east, although he worried that it would swing round to the north. Providence was on their side. They had timed their approach perfectly and were downwind of their quarry.

The hunt was on.

He heard a rustle at his shoulder and turned to see Prince Albert, face streaming with water, whiskers plastered to his skin. He lay prone, behind a peat hag, and held his rifle above the soaking vegetation.

'Well, McAdie? Is that my prize hart?'

'Aye, sir. We must be stealthy if we are to catch him.'

'I thought I saw another team of hunters. What if they are after the same animal?'

McAdie scanned the glen with his telescope a second time. 'You have good eyes. I cannae see anyone else.'

'Down there, near the ford.'

A gap in the clouds allowed McAdie to look down on the Falls of Tarf with greater clarity for a few seconds. Water churned through the gorge. He could see no sign of his son, or the pony; but sure enough, making their way along the road from the north were two men on horseback. From this range McAdie could not tell if they carried weapons.

'Who owns the land to the north?' the Prince whispered.

'The Earl o' Fife, who is away from home the now. They must be poachers.'

Isaac crept up to the parapet and squinted into the mist, scanning the scene below with great interest.

'I know how to deal with poachers,' the Jaeger said in a low voice.

In the old days poachers had been shot, hanged, or thrown in the river, but such practices were illegal in 1847, of course. McAdie wondered whether such barbarism was still practised in Bavaria. Firing a warning shot overhead was one thing, summary punishment quite another.

Isaac smiled grimly and made a throat-cutting motion that chilled McAdie's spirits far more than the wind and rain.

* * *

Few places were as familiar to Duncan as the Falls of Tarf. His earliest memory was of swinging on a birch tree above the waterfall while his mother fished in the river. He had climbed his sapling, swung away from the walls of the gorge, and whooped for joy as spray from the falls splashed against his skin. He couldn't have been more than three or four years old. Life had seemed simpler in those days: the sun shone with greater warmth, livestock had grazed the meadows by the water, and his father had smiled every day.

This place had grown desolate and hostile, far from the world of men and controlled by the whims of supernatural forces. The chasm roared with a million gallons of brown foam. Duncan's mother once told him that a witch lived in the ravine, who stirred up the waters when the spirits of the mountains were angry. Mosses and ferns trailed down the rock walls. The remains of an old bridge could be discerned on each side of the torrent: crumbling stone plinths just above the level of the waters. The old Duke had demolished the bridge nearly twenty years ago to discourage poachers from accessing Glen Tilt, and now the ford across the Tarf was a perilous wade through rapids.

Men frequently drowned here. Only a few years ago a group of vagabonds, making their escape after raiding Felaar Lodge, had been swept away with their cargo of wine casks and freshly shot harts.

The little meadow on the other side of the river had once been a garden of wild flowers, roamed by friendly cows with coats of red hair and horns as big as a stag's antlers. Now it was a midge-infested swamp. Rushes and moss had encroached from the mountain and taken over the neglected ground. The oak tree Duncan had climbed hundreds of times as a child had been killed by lightning five years ago and was now a rotting skeleton, of use only to the ravens who occupied the highest branches and watched travellers as they passed beneath.

Forbes leaned against his staff at the edge of the rapids. He had long ago given Duncan his knapsack to load onto the pony as he was incapable of carrying it himself. Although Lochain Lodge was less than a mile away, it had taken them almost an hour to get here and Forbes was clearly not tough enough for this journey.

'Onto the pony with ye, Professor,' Duncan said.

Forbes eyed the ford doubtfully. 'Must we cross here?'

'Aye, or trough through another two leagues of moss to the next ford.'

He took the Professor's staff and helped him up onto Floraidh's back. The pony did not complain at the added burden, but stepped fearlessly into waters that had overwhelmed greater beasts than she. Waves splashed high up her flank, inundating the baskets of sealed provisions.

Duncan followed across the ford. The cold water rose up to his chest and all but knocked the wind out of him, but he breathed deeply and ignored the bite, concentrating on placing his feet squarely and feeling for loose rocks with the staff. He leaned into the current. It sucked at him with a constant force, striving to pull his legs out from under him and drown him in the Tilt downriver.

Finally they struggled up the far bank and stood dripping by the pointed stone that marked the northern border of the reserve. This was the moment of parting. Duncan could not accompany the Professor for another step beyond the marker stone.

What would become of him? Now that the moment had come, the young ghillie felt torn in two. His duty to the estate was clear, and yet the Professor's increasingly feeble condition spoke to his conscience. Could he really abandon him to the harsh weather of the Mounth?

I have brought this man here. He is my responsibility.

Then he remembered his father's unsmiling face and the perilous line their family walked between secure employment and destitution.

'This is the border of the estate,' Duncan shouted above the noise of the falls. 'I must leave you here.'

Forbes dismounted from the pony and took back his staff. His thin hair was plastered over his forehead and the brim of his hat dripped with water. He looked pathetic, and yet when he raised his head and met Duncan's gaze something utterly relentless smouldered there: an indefatigable spirit, a power of will that could never be broken. Duncan took a step back. He had not yet seen this side to the sickly Professor's character.

'I need you,' Forbes said in a low voice. 'For pity's sake, how much do you want? I will pay any price you ask of me.'

Duncan said nothing for a long moment, for in truth this could be the escape ticket from Glen Tilt he had long sought.

'And your destination?'

Forbes was starting to shiver from cold. 'Bràigh Riabhach. I've come to study the ice corries to the north. What chance do you think I have alone out here?'

'Let me think for a moment, aye?'

I could ask for ten pounds. I could leave and make a new life for myself in Edinburgh.

Then he thought of his father, who had grown old and bitter waiting for the post of head keeper to fall vacant. He thought of his mother, who had suffered and worked hard for years but never complained. They deserved a better life just as much as he did. A little money would help only himself; he would need a fortune to help his entire family.

Or this could be my only chance to get away.

He opened his mouth to speak, but until the final moment knew not which way his spirit would lean. Some decisions are best left to the fates.

Before he could utter a word, a salvo of gunfire rained down from the mountain and echoed in the gorge. Fate, it seemed, had another game to play.

* * *

Forbes looked about himself in confusion.

'They're firing on us!'

Voices echoed in the ravine, rising above the din of the water. Another gun fired and the ball hit the ground ten paces away with a sharp *smack*. A horse whinnied somewhere close by, followed by a crash and a long, drawn-out clatter of loose rocks.

'Into the ravine while they reload!'

Forbes shrank back against the wall of the gorge, but Duncan climbed up onto the rocks to get a better view, hair flying loose in the spray, rifle in hand. He hurried to load the weapon and aimed it at the notch in the skyline where all the commotion was coming from.

'Stay right where ye are, Professor,' he shouted. 'I'll deal with this.'

Forbes kept well hidden in the growth of ferns beside the torrent. A horseman galloped over the brow of the hill. He was young, no older than Duncan, and dressed in drab riding clothes, slick with rain. He carried no rifle. Where, then, had the shots come from?

The horseman struggled to control his mount, which shied away from the rapids and snorted at the sight of Duncan's rifle.

To Forbes' surprise he realised that the newcomer was none other than his student Ewan Carr. He had lost the harried look of the youth who had turned up at Eastertyre only a few days ago, complaining of blisters and vicious gamekeepers. Now his demeanour was one of easy confidence and he sat upright in his saddle, facing the loaded weapon at point blank range.

'You there! Why did you fire on us?'

'I didnae shoot at ye, not yet anyway,' Duncan growled. 'State your business.'

'I am a student of the University of Edinburgh, and my business is my own.'

Forbes began to suspect that Carr had been drinking. His tone was confrontational, his words slurred.

Duncan kept his gun trained on the horseman. 'Aye, a likely story. You're a poacher.'

'Heaven preserve us from obstinate Highlanders!' Carr looked back up the hill and cupped a hand to his mouth. 'Professor Balfour! A ghillie is blocking our path!'

Forbes heard another horse moving down the loose path of scree and mud from the top of the ravine. A voice that Forbes recognised echoed close by:

'Carr! Stand down, for God's sake. We'll have no more shooting.'

Forbes knew the second horseman well. John Balfour, the Professor of Botany, spent nine tenths of his career in a greenhouse or a classroom—and yet he had the robust and powerful physique that Forbes had once possessed. He stood six foot six if he was an inch. Curly side-whiskers and a brisk smile completed the visage that Forbes was used to seeing looking through a magnifying glass at some preserved specimen of exotic lily.

Forbes chose this moment to emerge from the vegetation and meet the travellers. Their eyes turned on him and for a moment he felt self-conscious. Meetings between academic men usually took place in civilised places where all were decently attired and most certainly not dripping with water and covered in bits of dead bracken.

Carr had dismounted and now stood beside his horse, patting her flank. His angry expression broke into a smile.

'Professor Forbes! Well, bless me. It seems my tales of glaciers and monsters stoked your curiosity after all!'

Balfour puffed through his substantial moustaches and added his own greetings. They shook hands while Duncan looked on, puzzled. He kept his gun trained on the intruders.

'You know this man?' the ghillie demanded.

'He's my student, Ewan Carr, and this distinguished gentleman is a colleague from the University of Edinburgh. I'll vouch for them, my boy.'

Duncan had not the opportunity to reply, for at that moment a volley of loose stones tumbled down the hillside into the ravine, accompanied by a shout of warning and the crunch of boots on scree.

* * *

Alec McAdie looked through his telescope into the ravine below. Just what was happening down there? He could see his son holding the ford against two horsemen, but unless his eyesight was getting worse neither of the strangers carried a gun.

However, Isaac had fired the first warning shot and now the Duke's blood was up. This would not end well. McAdie felt it in his bones. The last thing the master wanted was an altercation with poachers, ruining the royal hunt on which so much depended for them all.

Auld Thomas lay on a flat rock to his left, squinting down the barrel of his decrepit old flintlock musket. He spat a curse in Gaelic.

'Waste o' time. The hart will be miles away by now, scared off by the shots.'

'Aye, but we must be patient. Let his Lordship deal with the trespassers first.'

The Duke led the way down the hill towards the Tarf water, followed closely by Isaac and Prince Albert himself. All seemed wound up with nervous energy and ready for a confrontation.

'Happen I see the muckle beastie after all,' Thomas said in a low voice, pointing to the hillside beyond the ravine. 'Take a look.'

McAdie trained his telescope on the far hillside. Sure enough, a huge stag was slowly picking his way between the pools, oblivious of the drama unfolding below.

* * *

Duncan knew he had lost control of the situation the moment the horsemen turned up.

The original plan had been simple enough: send Professor Forbes on his way and wait by the bridge for his father as instructed. Then he had grown doubtful of the right course, and now the gorge was thronging with angry people and horses and all he could do was hold his ground on the rocks and wait to see what happened next.

He kept his gun trained on Carr and Forbes, who glared back at him accusingly. Well, what else was he to do? He did not trust the arrogant youth who had all but ridden him down. His breath stank of whisky and there was a dishonest look in his eyes.

The Duke of Atholl charged down the far bank and started wading across the torrent, holding his rifle high to save the powder. A stranger in a foreign outfit followed close on his heels, and finally a man who stepped awkwardly over the jumbled stones of the hillside—unmistakeably someone who was not at home among the mountains. From the quality of his clothing and the silver trimmings on his rifle Duncan identified him as Prince Albert. There was an angry gleam in his eye; clearly he was not amused at the interruption of his hunt.

The Duke climbed up the near bank and took aim at Ewan Carr, squinting down the barrel in his peculiar way to compensate for the poor sight in his left eye. The lad stepped back and raised his hands. Forbes, who stood next to him, tightened his grip on his staff. Duncan hoped there was not going to be a proper fight.

'What do you mean by showing yourself here a second time?' the Duke barked, voice trembling with aristocratic fury.

'We meet again, Murray.' Carr showed his open palms to demonstrate he carried no weapon. His smile was sly. 'We intend simply to pass through Glen Tilt and be on our way. This is not the first time I have been threatened and attacked on your land, and I tell you I will not stand for it.'

'You impudent dog! There is no right of way here, and to make matters worse you have interrupted a royal hunt. I suffer nobody to trespass on my reserve!'

In truth, Duncan had not expected the Duke to confront the strangers quite so vehemently. Perhaps he was trying to demonstrate his authority in front of Prince Albert. On the other hand, it was obvious that this youth was already known to the Duke.

Professor Balfour stepped in front of Carr, drawing himself up to his full height. 'For God's sake, man, this isn't 1745! I'm here to collect plant specimens. Look!' He reached up to open one of his saddlebags and pulled out a handful of leaves pressed between handkerchiefs. 'D'you see now?'

The Duke was about to reply when the foreign Jaeger lowered his gun and pointed past the group at something on the hillside beyond.

Damh-mor!

The great hart stood not a hundred yards away, next to the cloven rock by the pool. His coat was streaked black with peat, matted into a grotesque mane that hung down from a neck as thick as a tree trunk. His antlers cast a magnificent silhouette against the rainclouds beyond: a spread of fourteen tines, sharp as spears and wider than a man's armspan. This wild creature was the largest stag Duncan had ever seen. Damh-mor stood as tall as a man and weighed as much as a pony. He was the jewel of the Atholl estate and would be the prize of a lifetime for any man who could catch him.

Ewan Carr chose the moment of distraction to make his escape.

'To me, Forbes! Balfour, ride like hell!'

All heads turned. Carr pulled a pistol out of his pocket and fired a shot in the air, then jumped back onto his horse and reached down to help Forbes get on behind him. In seconds pandemonium had broken out once again. Duncan saw the Professor clinging to Carr's waist as the young man spurred his horse up the bank to safety.

'Stop them!' the Duke shouted, brandishing his gun as if it were a walking stick. 'Will somebody fire on them, damn you all! Duncan, do your duty or by God—'

Duncan shook his head and stood firm. 'I'll nae shoot at a fleeing man.'

'Isaac! Stop them!'

The German Jaeger nodded. In a swift movement he raised his gun and let off a shot in the direction of Carr and Forbes. Smoke filled the close air of the ravine and the blast echoed above the noise of the churning water.

The shot appeared to miss, but the damage had already been done. Damh-Mor had disappeared.

In the confusion that followed Professor Balfour took his chance to get away. Hooves struck sparks on rocks, his horse plunged into the river and struggled to the far bank, and in the chaos Duncan saw Isaac firing another shot into the rapids.

Duncan heard Forbes crying over the noise: 'Wait, Carr! We must go north. I beg you, turn north!'

'Yes, we'll split up, that'll confound them! Happy hunting, Balfour!'

The last Duncan saw of Forbes was an accusing glance that cut the young man to his very soul. He had done his duty for the estate, of that there could be no doubt; why, then, did he feel so wretched? He knew deep down that he had betrayed the sickly Professor. At least he had not shot him in the back.

The horsemen galloped away: Balfour south into Atholl, Carr and Forbes north into Mar. The Duke bellowed in frustration and smote the boundary stone with the stock of his rifle.

'Damned insolent blackguards!'

Then he saw Duncan, still holding his position on the rocks. He took three steps towards him and seized his collar, shaking him over the rapids, a wild look in his eye.

'What do you mean by defying me, boy? You should have fired!'

'I'll risk the noose for nobody's sake but my own, your Grace,' Duncan replied, returning the glare. 'Have you forgotten that I stopped them crossing?'

The fury in the Duke's eyes faded, and he released his grip. 'Be that as it may, you have disobeyed me.'

Prince Albert had been conferring with Isaac, but now stepped up to the Duke. He looked like a man about to take control of the situation.

'We have a little sporting problem, do we not?' he said in a crisp German accent. 'The stag has run north, and one of the men who has defied us has gone south. Both must be apprehended.'

'Sir,' the Duke began after a deep breath, 'I have no right to put you in more danger. We must return to the castle immediately. I can only apologise, and trust that this minor incident has not in any way—'

Albert cut him off with a shake of his head. Duncan wondered if the Prince was angry with his host for allowing this calamity to take place, or if he was simply trying to make the best out of the situation.

'We will not return to the castle. Is this not my hunt? Did you not promise me the champion hart? I am not in the habit of giving up so easily!'

'But I cannot guarantee you will be back within the day if you go further north.'

'To the devil with returning within the day! I will have my prize; do you hear me, Murray?'

The Duke nodded mutely. 'As you wish,' he finally muttered, his authority undermined by the royal consort.

'Then I propose you follow the intruder south with Isaac and the old forester Thomas. I shall take the McAdies north to find my hart.'

'What of the horsemen who went north? I think Isaac should go with you. You might need his … protection.'

A look passed between Isaac and the Duke.

'If they truly are poachers, then I shall deal with them myself. Isaac will go with you, Murray, and perhaps reflect on his recent deeds. I do not approve of shooting at human beings.'

'I must protest—' the Duke attempted a second time.

'Enough! I no longer require Isaac's presence on this hunt.'

Duncan could see no remorse in Isaac's eyes. He looked oddly triumphant for a servant who had just been reprimanded by his master.

* * *

'I think I've been shot,' Carr gasped. 'My foot hurts like the devil.'

In a curious way, Forbes was enjoying himself. The confrontation at the ravine had put a strain on his nerves at first, and he still had no clear notion of exactly what had transpired back there, but the thrill of the chase made him feel alive again. Wind and rain in his hair had put the colour back into his cheeks and the pain in his side diminished with every yard they galloped north. He felt a little more like his old self.

Now, however, the horse was faltering and Carr winced with every jolt. They stopped by a bend in the river. The glen had closed in as they travelled upstream, rising as abrupt slopes of heather and scree on either side of the river. Forbes looked about him nervously. What if they were being followed?

As he helped his student dismount Forbes was alarmed to see that Carr's face had turned very pale. The horse quivered where she stood. A great streak of blood mingled with the rainwater that washed down the animal's side.

It did not take long to determine that the source of the blood was Carr's left foot. One side of his boot had been blown off by a rifle ball. So much blood pulsed from the wound that it was impossible to tell where the shoe leather ended and the young man's flesh began.

'Merciful Lord!'

'Give me some whisky,' Carr demanded through clenched teeth.

Forbes administered the liquor and immediately set about removing Carr's boot, a process hindered by his frequent oaths and pleas not to aggravate the wound. The sock was completely saturated in blood, but after it had been removed Forbes saw that the injury was not as bad as supposed. The boot had absorbed most of the force from the ball. The side of his foot was badly cut, but Forbes could find no evidence of broken bones. If infection could be avoided it would heal readily enough.

'What you need is a tourniquet. Do you have a blanket?'

'In the saddlebag.'

After cleaning the wound and dabbing on a little alcohol, Forbes washed a clump of sphagnum moss in the river and bound it to Carr's foot with a strip of cloth from the blanket. The bleeding diminished after a few moments although the wrapping would probably have to be changed in an hour or two.

Carr swore fluently throughout the process. 'Damn him to hell! Can you believe it? I'll have the Duke of Atholl in court for this. This is meant to be a civilised country!'

Forbes could not help but reflect that shots had been fired by both parties, but he kept that observation to himself. Carr had acted rashly, and to make matters worse had apparently enjoyed the confrontation. It was becoming clear that his young friend had a very immature notion of adventure.

'Do you think you can bear to put your boot back on?'

'Is there any point? I shan't be able to walk anyway—ouch! Careful, damn you!'

Forbes laced the boot tightly. It was probably a pointless gesture, considering the huge hole in one side, but it would help to protect the injury while it healed. They were a long way from help, after all

They looked at each other. Carr's angry expression suddenly dissolved into laughter, and once again they were Professor and student, sharing a pot of tea after a lesson.

'Ah! What a silly thing to happen. Sorry I spoke to you like that, Professor.'

'It's quite all right, my boy. I dare say you have never been shot before.'

Carr shook his head, serious once again. 'Will they come after us?'

Forbes considered the question. Albert had a reputation as a fair ruler, but he was also a sportsman who had been denied his quarry. The Duke had been challenged by trespassers and made to look like a fool who had no control over the borders of his own estate. Yes, they would be pursued, especially if the huge stag had moved north as well.

'We could head east to Castletown of Braemar,' Forbes suggested. 'It's the closest route to medical help.'

Carr was already shaking his head. 'No! I could not bear it. You have been through hell to get this far, that much is clear, and ... well, damn it, I feel responsible. If it wasn't for my foolish little stunt back there at the fords you would be well on your way towards Bràigh Riabhach by now.' He grinned sheepishly. 'This is my fault.'

'But you need to get that wound looked at.'

'It's only a graze, and you have patched it up admirably. Let's have a proper adventure together, eh Professor? I always did yearn to go to the Alps with you and be an explorer. I ... look here, I can't quite face going back to the real world just yet. D'you take my meaning, sir? Besides, think what a tale this will make.'

Forbes paid little attention to the boy's nervous prattling. It was quite obvious that he was concealing some fact, and had a strong aversion to travelling south; but at this stage Forbes was more concerned with the future. What if they were followed by the Duke's men? He would receive no quarter from Duncan McAdie, of that he was quite certain; the young ghillie had demonstrated where his loyalties lay. Forbes worried about his own weakness and the wellbeing of his injured companion. It would be a long road north with no comfort to be found at the end of it.

He found himself smiling despite it all. For the first time in five years he felt truly alive again.

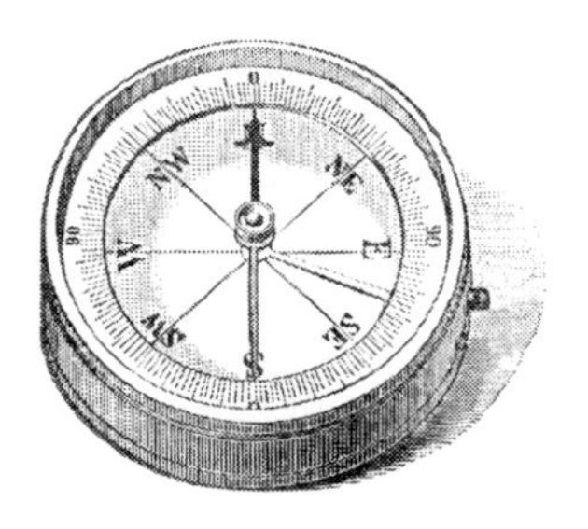

CHAPTER IV
A BEAUTIFUL MONSTER

THE CHEST OF DEE COULD BE A CRUEL PLACE for the Cairngorm traveller. Situated halfway between Blair Atholl to the south and Glen Spey to the north, this flat river plain was far from any settlement and was exposed to the full force of the arctic winds that blasted down from the Cairngorm plateau. Today the wind drove the rain before it and whipped the surface of the river Dee into a frenzy of crested waves and flying spray. A few old trees clung to the riverbank, shivering and moaning with every gust. Land and sky merged into a blend of iron grey and dun brown.

McAdie had not journeyed this far into the territory of Mar for some years. Deer frequently moved between estates, and the lairds had a gentleman's agreement that harts could be chased into neighbouring lands on a hunt—provided none of the other estate's animals were shot. This accord had served the land well for nearly a century, but in all McAdie's long years in service he had never chased a beast this far into a neighbouring estate. Damh-mor was no ordinary stag, and this was no ordinary stalk.

Deer could be seen picking their way across the hillsides from time to time, but none of these were the hart they pursued.

The hunters crouched in a hollow behind a rampart of peat, taking on refreshment before the next stage of their journey. McAdie crunched an oatcake and swilled it down with a draught of whisky. Prince Albert dined on the richer food Duncan had brought up with him on the pony from town: cold roast fowls, cheeses, and a bottle of claret.

Floraidh herself lay on a patch of grass a little distance away, snorting peacefully in the rain.

Duncan was unusually silent. McAdie worried about his son constantly these days, and all his worries seemed to focus on one question: would he stay in Glen Tilt, or would he follow so many other young people to the big cities in the quest for employment? Why did the youngsters not stay at home as they had done in the old days, learning a trade and settling down, honouring their traditional way of life? It seemed to the old forester that the world had turned upside down. He only hoped his son would choose to stay in the Mounth of his own accord.

'What's bothering ye, son?' he asked after a little while, speaking in Gaelic to mask the conversation from Albert.

Duncan looked up. There was a haggard look in his eyes, a rawness, as if he had undergone a great trial. 'What happened back there at the ravine wasnae right.'

McAdie looked sidelong at the Prince, who was eating heartily and paid no attention to his servants. 'The master commands and we obey. That's the way it has always been. Besides, who are we to tolerate poachers trespassing on the estate?'

Duncan simply shook his head, unable to meet his father's eye. McAdie's concern for his son hardened to a knot of anger. If the lad was going to be obstinate then perhaps he deserved whatever fate had in store for him.

Albert had put his food to one side and was scanning the horizon with a spyglass.

'Ich kann einen Hirsch sehen!'

McAdie's ears pricked up at the words. *Hirsch* meant stag, he was sure of it.

After hours of tramping through sodden moorland the Prince looked just as bedraggled as the rest of them, and

McAdie reflected that perhaps there was some truth in the old saying that Nature was the great leveller. The stern efficiency with which he had dismissed the other members of their party had evaporated just as quickly as it had appeared, and now he was back to his polite, amiable self, quietly taking orders from McAdie as he manoeuvred the group.

McAdie put his flask of whisky back in his pocket and extended his telescope, joining the Prince at the rampart. Albert gave him a clap on the back and pointed out over the moor. McAdie twisted the barrel of his telescope to bring the landscape into focus.

Damh-mor was grazing beside a torrent coming down from Beinn MacDuibh. The mountain's snow-clad bulk did not show through the cloud, but McAdie knew it would be there: an undulating plateau reaching up to heaven, peppered with granite and harbouring a dozen secret places where snow survived all year round. The great hart munched at a fern growing to one side of a waterfall. He raised his head, perhaps at a noise or a scent on the wind, and shook the water from his mane. His body tensed in readiness for instant flight and he scanned the landscape with wary eyes for some moments before returning to his feast.

'We must be careful if we are to bring him to bay,' McAdie whispered. 'The wind has turned. He has the advantage, and if he smells us he will fly north without stopping for fifty miles.'

Albert stroked his moustaches. 'Why north?'

'The beasts always run upwind when pursued. Duncan, get the pony ready. We shall need wings if we are to catch him.'

Duncan took no interest in proceedings. He crouched on the grass next to Floraidh, teasing some of the mud out

DUNCAN MCADIE

of her coat. He muttered something under his breath and made no effort to get up.

McAdie took a step towards the lad and made a fist with his right hand. 'Get up, I say! If you continue to disobey me—'

'What? What'll ye do, father … beat me in front o' the Prince here? I'm a grown man!'

McAdie shook his head. He felt weary of the whole business. His life was out here on the mountains, and a royal hunt was a moment of great pride for him, even under such circumstances. Why could his son not see that? Did he care nothing for his family, for his life of service to the Atholl estate?

Now was not the time for this conversation, although McAdie had no doubt that the fight would come soon enough. He dreaded the moment when his son would finally assert his independence and leave Lochain Lodge forever. Perhaps he had not always treated Duncan with tenderness—truth be told, he was not a tenderhearted man—but everything he had done was with the lad's best interests in mind. The argument would tear his family apart when it came.

For now he simply required his son to do his duty. He took hold of Duncan's collar and hauled him to his feet.

'Do your job, son. We'll talk when this is over, ken?'

Duncan's eyes were full of doubt, but after a moment he nodded.

'Stay at least a hundred yards behind us with the pony. We cannae risk the hart catching her scent.'

Albert had already left the cover of the peat rampart and was crawling through the heather ten paces away. McAdie caught up rapidly and took the lead.

'Do not lose my prize for me, McAdie,' the Prince said in his genial way, but in his words McAdie heard the threat of ruin from the Duke.

* * *

Professor Balfour was worried his pony might be at the last of its strength. The poor beast had waded through bogs, forded rivers, endured gunshots at close range, and was now being ridden at an unsustainable pace down the length of Glen Tilt in miserable weather. The north wind drove them ever south. Hooves thundered over the road as they passed the bogs and poor grazing land north of Forest Lodge. Highland creatures flew in alarm at the noise of their approach: here a hind grazing by a fountain, there a hare springing across the road in one bound. The incessant rain had turned the road to a quagmire and Balfour's coat was drenched in mud thrown up from the pony's hooves.

They passed Forest Lodge in a blur. It was strange to see such a grand residence out here in the wild, but the landowners liked their comforts. Faces looked out from the windows as his pony jumped the gate on the far side of the compound.

Another mile took him past the ramshackle dwelling of Clachghlas, the last working croft in Glen Tilt. A man in a leather smock herded muddy sheep into a barn with no roof, while ponies tossed their heads and raced beside the road, easily overtaking Balfour.

Hearing a sound on the road behind him, he looked back. To his surprise, he was being pursued at close range by a horseman. *What the deuce? I thought the blackguards were on foot!*

'*Halten Sie!*' the stranger shouted.

Balfour pressed his heels into the pony's flanks, but the beast wheezed and slowed its pace, shaking its head obstinately. After a few moments of this grumpy behaviour it finally stopped altogether and stood in the lee of a stone wall, head down, looking sorry for itself. Rain dripped from the branches of a larch tree above.

The horseman caught up in seconds. He was a tall fellow with a cunning face and his mount was a handsome chestnut beast of about fifteen hands, energetic and lively; probably a fresh horse from Forest Lodge. Balfour recognised the foreigner as one of the men who had confronted him at the Falls of Tarf.

He took off his pointed hat and made a mocking little bow. He tapped the fingers of his left hand against the stock of a rifle, slung at his back, but the powder horn at his belt was soaking wet and Balfour wagered he had no dry powder to load the weapon with. Nevertheless, Balfour raised his hands in supplication.

'All right, sir, you have run me to the ground. What's your name? I'll need to know when I make my report to the magistrate.'

'I do not answer to poachers.'

'For Christ's sake give me your name!'

The man shrugged as if it was of little account after all. 'Isaac. I am in the service of his Royal Highness, Prince Albert, but I act with the full authority of George Murray, the 6th Duke of Atholl, on whose land you are trespassing.'

'A pass has existed through Glen Tilt since time immemorial. The Duke is wrong to prevent travellers from making use of it.'

'The excuses of poachers. No doubt you would also say that since men have hunted deer on this land since ancient times, you are justified in taking the Duke's beasts for your own table. You are all the same. I have caught a hundred like you in the Bavarian forests, and I have heard every clever story you could imagine.'

Balfour took a deep breath to calm himself, although he felt like exploding with anger and teaching this impertinent foreigner a lesson. 'I have no interest in deer. Good God! Do I sound like a poacher to you? I am Her Majesty's Botanist and keeper of the Royal Botanic Gardens in Edinburgh!'

Isaac actually smiled. 'Most amusing.' Now he unslung the rifle and held it loosely pointed at the Professor. 'You will lead your pony in front of me at a distance of ten paces, and if you attempt to escape then I will shoot you. *Ist das Klar?*'

Balfour didn't know what else he could say in the face of such obstinacy. He gritted his teeth, nodded mutely, and promised himself that when he reached Blair he would kick up an almighty stink. They said the Queen was staying at the castle. *Wait until I tell her what has befallen me!*

His thoughts turned to his colleagues, harried and hounded into the Forest of Mar. Alicia Forbes deserved to know how her husband had been treated.

* * *

As he had found so many times before, Forbes discovered that adversity sharpened his wits and strengthened his resolve. He may be hungry and far from the comforts of home and family, his clothes may be wet through from the rain and his feet chafing in his boots, but this was *life!* He had a purpose again, by God, and he would give every ounce of his spirit to the adventure.

They advanced by the side of the Dee. The river navigated a lazy course between ancient moraine ridges and heaps of stones deposited here thousands of years ago when the glaciers receded. The landscape changed as they paced out the miles. Gone were the undulating grouse moors of the Mounth, the swampy glens and the stands of pine; this was a far older and harsher realm, an Alpine environment in which signs of the ancient ice world could still be discerned. Heather gradually gave way to rock and banks of gravel.

Twenty years ago nobody had suspected that Northern Europe had once been crushed beneath a glacier truly colossal in size. This plate of ice was sufficiently massive to depress the surface of the Earth and pulverise entire mountain ranges, carve deep glens through the land and deposit vast quantities of debris over every landscape from the far north of Scotland to the plains of Norfolk. It was a geological event of cosmic scale. Forbes had helped to discover the evidence in favour of the theory, building on the pioneering work of his European colleagues Charpentier and Agassiz.

Agassiz. His fingers curled into a fist. *The devil who stole my work and claimed it for his own, tried so hard to ruin me!*

That bitterness was in the past now, for in the end his relentless nature had ground Agassiz down in turn; yet the taint of the feud still lingered, and his reputation would never be free of it. People still looked at him and thought, "That man has stolen the work of another." How wrong they all were—how much Forbes would dearly wish to be free of it!

An ice age! What a remarkable notion.

The theory still troubled him, for where in the story of Creation was an ice age mentioned? He believed in the Almighty Architect who had first constructed these mountains, but sometimes scientific theories challenged his religious sensibilities. Perhaps at the end of his road he would find another piece of the puzzle.

He walked beside Carr, who sat astride the horse and sang old Jacobite songs, tunes he had picked up in the Edinburgh gin palaces, and even a song from the Atholl estate:

If to Felaar we do march off,

As I muckle dread we may;

Some Atholl Brose afore we go

Angus and I shall hae!

The journey's long and rugged too,

Some waters for to cross;

Some hills to climb, but worst of all

Is troughing through the moss.

When at the castle we arrive

How pleasing 'tis to see

At night the harts and birds come home

In dozens two or three.

Alec McAdie spies out the harts,

My Lord Duke does shoot them;

Duncan he does bring them home,

And Angus he does cook them.

He laughed when he had finished the song, and Forbes laughed too. It was amusing to hear an old hill song from the mouth of a wealthy student whose accent was quite different from that of the Highlanders who worked the land.

'Where did you hear that, my boy?'

'At Pitlochry. I spoke to a former Atholl forester who had recently been thrown out by the Duke. He told me how to gain access to Glen Tilt from the north and warned me to keep my head down. Ha! I've given the Duke the slip twice now.'

Forbes frowned. He felt bound by duty to give some advice to his young student.

'The Duke's men were wrong to shoot at us, but you did everything you could to provoke them! "To err is human; to forgive, divine."'

Carr shook his head, and a little of the cavalier nature Forbes had witnessed at the falls crept back into his countenance. 'I don't easily forgive, sir. The Duke has not just made a fool out of me, he's also done a great wrong to one of your colleagues. A learned man like Balfour should not be hounded from place to place merely for carrying out his scientific work. Why, he has defied you as well!'

Forbes began to sense that he would not win this argument.

'For my part I bear no grudge. Why seek out conflict? You went back into Glen Tilt after you had been expelled the first time … and with a pistol in your pocket!'

Carr had the goodness to blush a little. The firearm weighed down the right-hand pocket of his jacket, and as he rode he often rested his hand there to check on the weapon. 'A sensible precaution under the circumstances.'

'And yet you are the one with a gunshot wound. Listen to me, my boy. You are to do exactly as I say from now on, do you understand? We must not seek out conflict with the masters of this land.'

Carr winced in pain and reached down to rub his foot through his boot. 'Yes, yes; of course,' he said testily after a moment.

Forbes hoped his student would obey his commands. Out here their relationship felt more equal and less constrained by the conventions of University life, but Forbes was still the senior man and he did not trust Carr if it came to another conflict.

* * *

Duncan had tried to keep the subject of the spectre out of his mind as they journeyed north. As the landscape changed, became more rugged and less friendly, he found his thoughts returning to the stories his mother had told him as a child: the Witch of Beinn a'Ghlo, the ghosts of Felaar Lodge, and the Bodach of Mar. As he grew up he had gradually learned that most of these legends had no truth to them, except one.

The Bodach of Mar is the true laird of these hills, and suffers no trespassers.

His father led their party at a ferocious speed up the southern flanks of Beinn Bhrotain, and Duncan had to work hard to maintain the hundred yard distance required. The rain had stopped about an hour ago, but now he was sweating from the exertion and his shirt felt itchy against his skin. They had long ago passed into the cloud. Every man in the party trusted Alec McAdie's instincts to guide them, for they had no map or compass and could see nothing beyond the swirling mist that enclosed them on all sides.

Floraidh plodded beside him, indefatigable as ever, hooves finding secure purchase in the mess of peat and scree underfoot. It seemed to Duncan that the animal occasionally looked about herself with greater awareness than he was used to seeing on her dumb face. It was said that the beasts could see beyond this world into the mysteries of the next. Did she sense something, he wondered?

He caught up with Albert. The Prince was struggling with the run up this steep hillside, and paused for a moment, bent double, panting like a dog. He looked up and smiled at Duncan.

'I will rest for five minutes, I think,' Albert stated.

Duncan didn't know what to say. Could he deny a royal instruction? On the other hand, the foresters were in charge on the hill, not the masters.

'Not if ye want to catch your prize, sir. Damh-mor will proceed up the Dee and go to soil in Glen Geusachan. If we cannae find a way to approach his flank we'll ne'er catch him.'

And that, Duncan added to himself, *is why we have to climb this damned mountain.* If they stayed in the glens they would be outsmarted by their target.

Prince Albert nodded. He stroked his moustache and stared uphill into the mist, trying to penetrate it with his gaze. 'How long until dusk?'

'Four hours. It can be done, unless…' He trailed off, unwilling to burden the Prince with his superstitions.

'Unless what?'

'Sometimes the mountains have the final word.'

The Prince's hard expression dissolved into a smile. 'Ah! Your wonderful Highland folklore. Please tell me more.'

They started moving again. Duncan wondered if the Prince was merely humouring him or if he had a genuine interest.

'A spectre haunts these mountains. They call him the Bodach of Mar. He is the herdsman of the deer who live in this estate and also laird of the ice corries to the north.'

'Herdsman of the deer? Is that why you think it will affect us?'

'Aye,' Duncan said grudgingly. 'The Damh-mor is his champion hart. He'll no give him up to us without a fight.'

They climbed in silence for a few minutes. Then Prince Albert suddenly stopped and turned to face Duncan. His expression was earnest and somehow humble, as if he had been affected by what the young Highlander had told him.

'I am very pleased that you and your father have shown such devoted service to me, even though I have started this hunt in ignorance of your culture. You shall be well rewarded when this is over, I promise you.'

Duncan touched his forehead without thinking. 'Sir.'

That was the end of their conversation, for Albert increased his pace to catch up with McAdie. His words had made a strong impression on Duncan. The incident at the Tarf water had shown a hard side to Prince Albert: quick to judge, efficient in making decisions, slow to forgive. However, now Duncan had seen that Prince Albert was sensitive to local customs and perhaps a very different kind of man than the Duke of Atholl.

He thought about the impending argument with his father. It would result in him leaving Glen Tilt and the Duke's employment, of that he was increasingly certain—but perhaps if he played his cards right Prince Albert could provide a recommendation.

* * *

Victoria wondered when Albert would be back from his hunt. In the early years of their marriage she had sulked when they spent time apart, but gradually she had come to realise that he needed these interludes of private time away from his family. Their fights had been ferocious in those first few years as he struggled to settle into a new life as prince of a foreign land. Victoria's world had been a succession of parties and balls, of staying up until dawn, of revelling in London society. It had taken time for Albert's calmer influence and love of the natural world to tame her wild spirit a little.

Seven years and five children later, their relationship was more harmonious and Victoria had learned to be a little less selfish and a little more giving. In his turn, Albert had stopped fighting her in political matters and had found his place as a reforming influence and champion for the poor. She also found that she listened to him more often on political matters nowadays, too.

Nevertheless, his hunting trips rarely lasted longer than a few hours. She had missed him this afternoon, and worried that he would not be back in time for the birthday celebrations she had organised for the 26th. A strict understanding existed between them that he would never be away on a hunt for more than a day.

The Duke of Atholl returned late that evening from his hunt, but Albert did not accompany him.

Victoria had spent the afternoon painting while her children played in the garden or amused themselves by running around the vast interior of the house, watched over by the nannies. She had found herself a convenient window facing north east, towards the peak of Carn Liath, which she had noticed on the drive from Ardverikie. The rain had cleared away an hour ago and the light lent itself more favourably to landscape painting, although the remarkable effect of sunbeam and rain failed to recreate itself for her convenience. As always, the process of applying paint to paper calmed her racing mind and helped her to relax.

She saw the Duke's carriage draw up in the courtyard at the front of the castle. The pony was splattered with mud from its hooves to the crown of its head, and every man in the party appeared to be similarly befouled by the Scottish weather. Victoria counted only four men in the group and could see no trace of Albert.

Where could he be? What if some disaster has befallen him?

She rushed down the grand staircase, a square spiral of vast proportions watched over by the portraits of dead ancestors (and, of course, the mounted antlers of many dead stags). Atholl Highlanders stood to attention at every landing and gallery, and as her skirts whispered over the floorboards of the entrance hall a maid turned hurriedly to face the wall, feather duster in hand.

'Don't turn away from me, girl! Where is the butler?'

The girl turned, blushing furiously, and mumbled something unintelligible. The Queen guessed the lady of this house must treat her servants in rather an old fashioned way.

The butler arrived of his own accord, bowed deeply to Victoria—she could all but hear his elderly knees creak—and scolded the chambermaid.

'The hunting party has returned, Ma'am, although I fear without a single hart to show for their labours.'

'Open the door, Samson.'

He bowed again and did as commanded. The front door of the castle swung open with a groan of old hinges, and on the other side Victoria saw the silhouettes of two guards keeping vigil beneath the cornice.

The Queen swept down the steps and out into the courtyard, closely followed by Samson and one of his footmen.

One of the Duke's foresters, an elderly fellow who walked with a stooped posture, was engaged with the task of emptying the wagon of provisions and seeing to the fatigued pony. The Duke stood to one side, looking back towards the mountains with a far-off expression in his face.

Isaac held a stranger at gunpoint. The man looked perfectly miserable—a sorry specimen of humanity—and yet something about him was familiar to Victoria. The man took a step towards the Queen and lifted a hand as if to point, but Isaac stopped him with a twitch of his rifle barrel.

The Duke turned to look at Victoria. He offered a stiff smile; gone was the confidence and hope of the previous day, to be replaced by a sort of hesitant terror.

'I regret that I do not bring his Royal Highness back to you tonight.'

'Where is he, Murray?' she snapped.

'He has taken two of my foresters north into the Forest of Mar. They pursue the champion hart, who was frightened away by some poachers.'

'Poachers!'

'Blackguards, Ma'am. Albert assured me that if he catches them they will be severely punished.'

Victoria scowled. She was not amused by her husband's antics. Albert knew very well that he was expected back this evening, and it was most unkind of him to spend a night out in the mountains away from his family. In an attempt to direct her peevishness away from the Duke (who was in truth not at fault here) she took a moment to study the prisoner they had brought back with them from Glen Tilt.

'Who is this man?' she demanded of Isaac, who held his rifle in a loose grip at his waist while he smoked a pipe.

The Jaeger clicked his heels together and bowed crisply. '*Meine Königin*, he is an accomplice of the devils mentioned by my lord Duke.'

The impression of familiarity strengthened as Victoria studied the prisoner. He was dressed in bedraggled travelling clothes and muddy boots, and to outward appearance was every inch a member of that nomadic class of scoundrels who wander from estate to estate, shooting and stealing, raiding hunting lodges for supplies, and making merry with stolen whisky.

He was staring at her. The Queen stared back.

Victoria knew that face, she was sure of it. Those eyes, sunk deep into their sockets, intelligent and imbued with self-assuredness, were not the eyes of a common vagabond. He wore thin mutton-chop whiskers and a curly little beard.

'What is your name?'

'I am John Ba—' he replied, but before he could finish Isaac slammed the butt of his rifle into the man's stomach, and he doubled over in pain.

'Do not lie to the Queen!' the Jaeger shouted at him, then turned to Victoria. 'He persists with the fiction that he is a gentleman. I am sorry that you should hear this.'

The poacher swore at his captor and looked up sullenly. Victoria turned away from the scene of violence.

'Set this man free at the border of the estate,' she commanded. 'We are satisfied he has been taught a moral lesson and has suffered enough for his crimes.'

Isaac looked uneasy. 'But he is a criminal. He must be brought before the magistrate.'

Victoria had never altogether trusted Albert's Jaegers. He had brought them over with him from Coburg before their marriage, and together with his German valets they were his most loyal servants. However, Victoria believed their loyalty extended only to the person of their master, and that they had no love for the British way of life—or for the mistress of the household in which they served.

'And I am your sovereign! Must I repeat myself, Isaac?'

He bowed once again and withdrew. As Victoria watched the hapless poacher driven before the barrel of Isaac's gun, she reflected that although much had been done to civilise the Highlands in the century since Culloden, it remained a land of very different laws and customs to her own beloved England.

The poacher fired one last accusing glance back at the Queen, and once again she was disturbed by a sensation of familiarity. *I am simply upset that Albert has not come back,* she reassured herself. *There is no reason why I should have seen that rascal before today.*

* * *

Forbes and his student picked a flat campsite at the fork in the river. Dusk spread gradually over the landscape, first filling the glens and hollows amongst the rocks, then occupying entire slopes, creeping up to the ridges and plateaux high above. The dense cloud that had shrouded the mountains all day now began to break and lift with the sunset. For hours Forbes had walked in a sepia world of greys and browns, slick with rain, but now colour gleamed from the heavens: first a sliver of blue, then a golden beam cast through the gap in the clouds to illuminate the far hillside. He perceived that this was not a monochrome world after all, but one of subtle hues and shades. Emerald green merged with the muted shades of the plateau, and the snowfields, which Forbes had seen as flat white without form or texture, gleamed like jewels.

To the north, the first bastion of the Bràigh Riabhach massif reared up like the hulk of an old warship. Gullies, noisy with water, seamed the cliffs. The landscape breathed and sighed all around them, shaking off the last of the storm and settling down for the brief northern night to come.

The adventurers managed to light a fire despite the damp surroundings. Carr found a cache of dry wood beneath a rock, perhaps left there by deer-watchers or poachers, and after a few false starts Forbes managed to use one of the percussion caps from Carr's pistol to set light to some gunpowder and shredded cloth. He added sticks and coaxed the flame into life.

Carr let out a whoop. 'Hurrah! Warmth at last!'

He hobbled over to the horse, using Forbes' staff as a crutch, and retrieved his saddlebag with the provisions. The horse snorted and grazed on the close grass of the riverbank.

'Don't get too excited, my boy. We must keep this fire discreet.'

Carr sat down on a comfortable rock with the help of Forbes, who took the opportunity to examine his student's injured foot. The wound still looked ugly but had not bled for hours. More importantly, it bore no trace of infection. It would heal.

'Still hurts like the devil,' Carr remarked. He attempted a breezy smile, but beneath his patter Forbes detected nervousness. 'This is a bit of excitement, though, isn't it? Must make a change from the Edinburgh lecture season!'

Forbes nodded and added a stick to the fire. He wished his companion would be silent. After the frantic pace of the day he now relished the sensation of peace that washed over him. He had not enjoyed a wild camp in the mountains for … how many years? Closing his eyes, he shut out the gathering darkness and let the sounds of the landscape absorb him: the roar of the river, the sizzle of the fire, the murmur of wind on distant heights. The contrast between the heat of the fire on his face and the chill of the evening on the back of his neck was delicious.

He opened his eyes again. Carr sat there on his rock, injured leg resting across one knee, holding his hands up to the blaze. Forbes thought he looked remarkably calm for a man who had been shot a few hours before. Their eyes met through the plume of smoke.

'Are you hungry, sir?'

Forbes craved tobacco more than food. 'Frankly I would give anything for a smoke. Do you have a pipe? I lost mine at the ford.'

Carr answered in the affirmative, and as they shared his pipe and prepared a meal of vegetable stew the sky grew darker and the world contracted to the circle of firelight and the curve in the river which encircled their campsite. Carr uncorked his bottle of whisky and they shared a dram together. They talked about old times and forgot about the vast reaches of wilderness stretching for many miles in all directions.

The bottle of whisky gradually got lighter, their speech grew louder and more merry, and Forbes felt the glow of alcohol on his cheeks.

'Tell me about the Bodach,' he said after an hour of stories and song.

Carr was silent and drew back out of the light of the fire, leaving his face in shadow. Forbes realised that he had broken the spell.

'I don't know very much apart from what I have already told you. Tell me about your plans for the survey of the mountain. I still have no clear idea how long it will take or how you plan to do it.'

'There's time enough for that later! Tell me about the monster. We are in his territory, are we not?'

Carr remained silent. All of a sudden Forbes was conscious of the nothingness all around them: an empty wild expanse of moor and mountain, rock and ice, governed by storms and the long geological processes he had devoted his life to studying. Above, stars gleamed down on them out of the firmament. It would be easy to believe in supernatural forces in a place like this. Forbes, of course, knew better; but he was amused that his student was so easily taken in by local superstitions.

Then he heard a sound over the ceaseless rush of the river. It sounded like a footstep.

Carr leapt upright, then yelped as his weight bore down on his injured foot.

'What was that, by God?'

Forbes helped him sit back down, alert all the while for another sound. He was acutely aware of the alcohol in his blood, muddying his senses and confusing his limbs; but he was also a scientist by nature, and knew how to make observations under the most trying circumstances.

Crunch.

There it was again! It sounded like the impact of two stones, or the impression of a boot in scree. Carr pulled his little pistol out of his pocket and fumbled with his powder horn, spraying half the powder down the front of his shirt before managing to get some into the barrel.

'Careful of the fire!'

Carr didn't reply. He rammed a ball down the barrel and pulled back the hammer, then aimed the piece into the darkness with a shaking hand.

'Show yourself!'

For a moment, nothing moved. Then the watcher stepped forward into the glow of the fire.

A magnificent stag stood not twenty paces away, regarding them calmly from atop a knoll beside the river. The firelight revealed him piecemeal: first the flanks of his legs, crusted with mud and scarred by fights with other harts; then his bovine head and the gleaming expanse of his antlers. Eyes glittered with a cunning that, it seemed to Forbes, transcended that of any animal. For a minute each watched the other, captivated: the Cairngorm resident and the intruders into this prehistoric landscape.

'It's the great stag again,' Forbes whispered. 'Do you think the hunters have followed him this far?'

'I don't know, but it's a damned shame,' Carr said, making no effort to lower his voice. 'Look at the brute. He's beautiful. I cannot abide the thought of anyone shooting him for sport—especially not that criminal of a Duke.'

'It's the way of the land, my boy.'

'Not if I can help it.'

With that, Carr raised his pistol and fired it vertically. The flash lit the stag's face with greater clarity for an instant, although he was too old, too calm, to be panicked. He took a step back but did not flee.

Carr cupped a hand to his mouth. 'Run, you beautiful monster!' he shouted as loud as his voice would permit. 'Run! Be free while you can!'

The beast lurched away and was gone.

* * *

Duncan took the first watch that night.

The hunters made their camp on a broad peak at the head of Glen Geusachan. Behind them lay the mountain ridge they had traversed from the summit of Beinn Bhrotain that evening; ahead, the snowy bulk of Bràigh Riabhach's southern flank. While the others lay wrapped in their blankets sleeping deeply after the hardships of the day, Duncan sat on the cairn and scanned the moonlit landscape with his father's telescope.

His father had promised that the weather would come good, and as usual he had been right. The cloud had lifted and dispersed as they climbed the final few yards to Beinn Bhrotain's summit. Prince Albert had expressed admiration for McAdie's navigational skills, and morale had risen in the party, thoughts of the Bodach forgotten. A fine sunset was a good omen for the next day's hunt. At dawn they would descend into the glen beneath and bag their prize.

However, Duncan had spied something very worrying. Down there, two miles to the east, he could see a tiny point of light down by the river.

Could it be poachers, deer-watchers from the Mar estate, or perhaps Forbes and his associate? Duncan didn't know, but suspected the latter. Poachers occasionally used the campsite at the confluence of the Allt Geusachan and the Dee, but it was prone to flooding and offered poor shelter; in bad weather they had more cunning bolt-holes, old bothies hidden in the ice corries to the north. Forbes, by contrast, may claim to be a mountain explorer but his knowledge of the land was very bad. Duncan believed that the campfire he could see through his telescope marked the location of Forbes' camp.

So, the frail Professor was making the voyage north after all. Duncan smiled. *Good for you.* He admired tenacity, and had no doubt that lesser men in such poor physical condition would have given up long ago.

Crack … craack … craaaack.

The echo of a gunshot reached his ears over the whisper of the cataracts coming down from Beinn Bhrotain. Someone was shooting down there! He wondered if it could be poachers after all before remembering that

Forbes' young companion carried a pocket pistol. That impertinent fellow had not endeared himself to Duncan.

Should I wake my father? What if they have frightened the hart away and denied Albert his prize?

On reflection, Duncan decided to let them sleep. Nothing could be done tonight; and in any case, if he told the others what he knew then there would be hell to pay. The last thing he wanted was for his father to discover that he had actually helped the intruders to get this far.

He folded the telescope with a snap and settled into his cold chair of stone, counting stars to keep himself awake. *I will miss these lonely nights on the mountain when I have gone*, he thought, and wondered if the stars shone so brightly in the cities where they said work was plentiful and a young man might make his mark on the world.

* * *

Alicia Forbes found that she could not sleep while her husband was away.

I should be used to it by now, she thought as she lay in bed, watching the shadows dance on the ceiling. She wondered what James was doing at this precise moment: enduring some lonely and cold bivouac out on the moors, in all likelihood. Her first and last prayer of every day was for him.

Sometimes she wondered at the stupidity of the man. He had the remarkable facility, unique to driven men of science, to ignore every warning of his body; to ignore the advice of physicians; in short, to completely put from his mind everything pertaining to the weaknesses of the self, and drive every ounce of effort into the pursuit of his goals.

James was an obsessive, and she did not understand his obsessions.

Being married to such a man, who might only be at home for half the year, was a constant challenge. She had been looking forward to this holiday at Eastertyre since Christmas—had been looking forward to a *family* holiday with them all together under one roof for two weeks—and yet James was not here. He had gone off on an expedition yet again. Not content to spend almost all of his life working in his study, James was now excluding his family at the very time he ought to be paying the most attention to them.

A sound at the front door cut through the silence of the night, and she sat upright in bed, ears straining to detect the cause of the noise.

A knock! Then: 'Madam Forbes, are you awake?'

* * *

Alicia's first thought on opening the door was that the house was about to be robbed. The rays from her candle illuminated a vagabond standing on the doorstep, shivering and clasping his arms to his chest. Eyes glimmered with anger and a deep fatigue. By the way he stood Alicia could tell that he had travelled a great distance on foot. Was he a common thief, or a reduced gentleman begging for pennies?

She shrank back into the porch, mindful of Eastertyre's isolation.

'Will you have the goodness to let me in, or am I to be turned away from every friend I thought I had in this God-forsaken county?'

His accent was that of Edinburgh, and Alicia recognised his voice immediately, despite the ragged clothes and layer of grime coating his unshaven face. *Surely it cannot be Professor Balfour, the esteemed colleague of my husband who has dined at our house on so many occasions?*

'Do you not recognise me?'

'John Balfour?' she whispered. 'What has happened to you? Come in, come in!'

She lit a few candles in the living room and settled him down before the fire, which had burned down from the evening before but still emitted a warming glow. Balfour sank into the armchair with a weary sigh and closed his eyes for a moment to collect himself. Alicia listened for any sign that her children had been disturbed by the visitor, but all was calm upstairs. The old house slept soundly.

Balfour opened his eyes and fixed her with a piercing stare. In that look she detected a righteous indignation at whatever misfortunes fate had piled upon him. She found herself frightened by that expression, and for a wild moment wondered if she had been mistaken, and had brought a robber into her house after all.

'Would you like some tea?' she said quickly, to cover her disquietude.

He swept the question aside with an impatient shake of his head. 'I bring news of your husband.'

Alicia gasped involuntarily and sat down. Instantly she feared the worst.

'Tell me where he is.'

'Riding north from the Tarf water. There was another dispute with the Duke and his men. Forbes and his student rode north into the Cairngorms, but they are being pursued by Prince Albert.'

'Why?'

Balfour gave a bitter laugh. 'They disturbed a royal hunt and chased away a hart. The landowners think we are all poachers. Good God! I myself was chased for ten miles before being captured and escorted to the border of the estate. The Queen didn't even recognise me in my sorry condition. Think of that, Mrs Forbes!' He closed his eyes and gave another long, ragged sigh. 'I didn't know where else to go. Even the innkeeper at Pitlochry turned me away.'

Alicia could hardly believe what she was hearing. To think that professional men from Edinburgh should be accused of poaching and chased by armed men across the countryside! That such things should happen in the year 1847! Balfour's tale stirred her own anger, and despite her grievances she felt a fierce loyalty for her husband at that moment and knew she would do anything to put right the wrong that had been done.

'You saw the Queen herself?'

Balfour nodded. 'She is staying at Blair Castle while Albert acts like a hothead out on the hunt. I fear for the consequences if it comes to a confrontation with your husband.' He managed a weak smile. 'Forbes is not a man to be browbeaten by anyone.'

Alicia rose again and warmed her hands by the fire, then immediately felt guilty. *James will not have a fire to keep him warm, out there on the moor.* Suddenly angry, she turned to Balfour. 'Were you aware that James is seriously ill? How dare you come back here without him!'

'Quite frankly, madam, I spoke to him for two minutes at most before we were fired upon. Forgive me. I think I can stay awake no longer.'

With that, Balfour closed his eyes and drifted into a profound slumber from which Alicia had not the heart to wake him for further interrogation. She drew a blanket around his shoulders and set a pitcher of water on the table beside him.

I must act. Since my husband is so clearly incapable of rescuing himself, I must be the one to do it.

She made preparations to leave at first light. After writing a letter for the governess and the maid, she packed a bag and laid out her travelling clothes. Her walking boots, which James had bought for her three years ago for their Alpine honeymoon, were a little scuffed after several walking tours but the hobnails were still bright and not too worn down.

Next she wrote a note to her daughters explaining where she had gone, and finally she chewed her pen as she thought about whether or not to write a letter to the Queen. Would it be better to present her with a letter or to ask to speak to her in person? Just what was the etiquette in cases like this?

She rubbed her tired eyes. *I am about to tell the Queen that Prince Albert is chasing my husband across the mountains. There is no etiquette for this situation.*

CHAPTER V
BRÀIGH RIABHACH

THE SUN DOES NOT TRULY SET during a Scottish summer night. At these northern latitudes, it merely dips below the horizon for a few hours, generating a twilight of extraordinary length and clarity. All but the strongest of the stars are chased from the heavens. When once again the sun rises in the early hours of the morning, it bursts forth with a silent fanfare of colour and warmth to drive back the chill of the night before. To the man sleeping wild under the sky it feels as if he has been asleep for hardly any time at all, until he is used to it. The adventurer sits himself upright with bleary eyes, swatting at the midges which have already come out to feed.

By the time the first rays of dawn showed on the mountain slopes that morning, Forbes and Carr had already been on the road for nearly an hour.

'A little more whisky, Professor?'

Forbes shook his head. 'Good heavens, no; not at this o'clock. Where have you managed to find another bottle?'

'In the saddlebag. What we lack in decent food we must make up for in cheer!'

Carr knocked back another dram of the local spirit, and Forbes reflected that his young friend seemed to be doing everything in his power to justify the insults Edinburgh citizens frequently directed towards the students of the city. Carr did not care that he was injured, or that the nearest inhabited place was ten leagues to the north, or that the Duke's irate ghillies were probably still chasing them. He was drunk and didn't give a damn.

Forbes kept one eye on the road and another on the landscape. The track they now followed was barely suitable for a horse, and progress was slow as Carr's mount clambered over rocks, struggled through tick-infested heather three feet deep, and plunged into sucking peat bogs.

On the other hand, the unfolding view of Bràigh Riabhach to their left was stupendous, and he frequently stopped to make notes and sketches in his pocket book.

This mountain was huge, at least as broad as Ben Nevis, the highest peak in Scotland, which Forbes had circumnavigated earlier in the year. That first bastion of crag beneath which they had made their camp—a veritable Matterhorn in its own right—proved to be the smallest and least remarkable peak in the range. Summit after summit reared up in rugged slopes from the Dee, each rising as a graceful form against the blue of the morning sky. Ridges, born in a confusion of rocks in the high corries, narrowed and converged to define four individual pinnacles stretching northwest for several miles. All looked distant and difficult to climb, although in the morning sunlight they were more inviting than the bog and heather through which they stumbled on their way to the ice corries further north.

After the hard miles he had walked to reach this point, Forbes was looking forward to finally being able to begin the scientific work he had come all this way to carry out.

* * *

Queen Victoria had not slept well last night, but after waking up with a headache and a temper she resolved to think nothing but tender thoughts about Albert until he should feel inclined to return.

'Visitors to see you, Ma'am.'

She looked up from her book. The time was not yet eight in the morning, and she was resting after a full breakfast, in preparation for a day out of doors. None of her children were up yet. Eight years ago she would hardly have gone to bed at this time, but Albert favoured early rising, and she had adopted the habit from him.

Albert has stayed out on the hunt overnight. He has broken his promise. She caught herself thinking unkindly about him, and forced a smile.

She loved this time of day. The sun began to climb in a sky of dazzling blue (so rare for an August day in the Highlands!) and the castle rooms, designed to make the most of what little light was usually available, seemed extraordinarily light and airy. A piper played a tune outside in the gardens.

'At this o'clock?'

Victoria was cautious of uninvited callers. She had survived a number of assassination attempts during the first few years of her reign, and even if the persons who wished to see her had no murderous intent, there existed a certain class of fawning parasites who had nothing better to do with their time than gawp at the royal family and beg for favours.

'Tell them that on no account will I see them,' she declared, turning her attention back to her book. 'I am on holiday and will receive no-one without an invitation.'

'He said you'd say that, Ma'am.'

She turned a page. 'And?'

'He said if you were to say that I should give you this letter.'

She sighed. 'Give it to me, then!'

She tore open the seal and scanned the few hurried lines inscribed therein. Certain she had not understood it, she read the note again.

What does this mean?

'Show them in at once.'

* * *

The guards escorted the visitors in to see her. Victoria thought they made an odd pair. The woman was young and pregnant; possibly a little younger than Victoria herself, although something about her posture, the way she held her head up high, suggested a mature bearing and experience beyond her years. Victoria also guessed that she was already a mother. She was pretty in an unsophisticated sort of way, and wore a plain travelling gown and white bonnet with a green ribbon.

Her expression conveyed a blend of emotions: some anger, a little determination, and a great deal of nervousness. She held her fists clenched at her side.

The gentleman was instantly familiar to her. This was the fellow who had been dragged out of her sight by Isaac last night. He had cleaned himself up a little, was no longer unshaven or caked with mud, but there could be no mistaking that look of indignation in his eyes. Now that he was standing upright in the drawing room of Blair castle, she could immediately tell that her first instinct had been correct: this man was no poacher. He was, in fact, Her Majesty's Botanist and keeper of the Royal Botanical Gardens in Edinburgh.

'What is the meaning of this note? How dare you accuse Albert of such a thing?' she demanded, skipping any pleasantries.

Balfour, in his turn, did not bow or make any sign of subservience. 'You do recognise me now, then. Did you recognise me last night in the courtyard?'

Victoria said nothing for a moment. Her blood was boiling after that note (Albert would never do such a thing, of that she was satisfied), and yet it occurred to her that she had done this man a grave disservice.

It went against the grain to be calm in the circumstances, but she decided that a less furious approach would be more appropriate.

'No, I confess I did not recognise you then. Will you sit down, both of you?'

They did as instructed. The woman sat on the very edge of a chair as if frightened to put her full weight on such an expensive object. She looked anxiously out of the window, at the red silk walls, down at her feet, unsure of where to look next. She fidgeted with the hem of her dress.

Victoria smiled at her. 'When is the baby due?'

Mrs Forbes started. Her face was very pale. 'Oh! About Christmas, we think, your Majesty.'

She spoke in a small voice, and Victoria wondered if she was simply awed at being in the presence of her sovereign, or if something else was bothering her.

'Your husband must be very proud. Who is he?'

'Professor James F—Forbes.' Her eyes filled with tears and she reached up to wipe her eyes, stoically avoiding the impulse to cry. 'Forgive me, your Majesty.'

'Hush, now! Don't call me that again; we are not at court here. Ma'am will do perfectly well.'

'Yes, Ma'am. I must beg your forgiveness for bothering you about this, but you see—well, my husband is very ill and…'

'Gad!' Balfour interjected, unable to contain himself for a moment longer. 'If you will not spit it out then I shall do so. Ma'am, as a member of your Royal household it is my duty to inform you that your husband has been misled by the Duke's men, and is at this moment hounding my colleague—the husband of this poor lady!—north into the mountains. Like myself, Forbes has been mistaken for a poacher. *A poacher!* We are scientists, Ma'am, not criminals, and this is the second time I have been persecuted while attempting to travel through Glen Tilt. The situation is intolerable and I will be taking legal action against the Duke of Atholl the moment I return to Edinburgh.'

Balfour folded his arms and sat back, mouth compressed to a frown. He had fired his broadside and now waited for the return volley.

Victoria looked at him in astonishment. Never before had she been spoken to like this by a commoner. Why had she not had the sense to turn them away? Once her indignation had abated a little, she began to ruminate on the consequences of what Balfour told her, if it were true. She had observed the botanist's mistreatment with her own eyes and blamed herself for not recognising him last night. There could be no doubt that Isaac had acted cruelly, possibly on Murray's orders.

As for the rest of it—well!

If Albert is at fault here, then he has been misled. He would not commit such an evil act of his own volition.

She was conscious of the blind spot Albert's faults occupied in her vision. She knew he sometimes acted in ways she did not approve—like the time he brought a dead stag into their bedroom for a joke—but she had the ability to overlook these little incidents and not allow them to tarnish the golden image of her husband. So long as he did what he was told, he was an angel.

Nevertheless, sometimes he needed a little guidance. Perhaps now was one of those times.

She looked at Mrs Forbes, who seemed to be balancing on the verge of tears. The poor woman's distress was palpable and eclipsed all other concerns in Victoria's eyes. She may be the Queen of Britain, she may play with politics and make or break governments, but she was also a wife and a mother. If Albert were in the situation of this woman's husband she would do anything to help him.

She smiled at them both.

'I think perhaps it would be a shame to waste this beautiful weather. I feel like a drive into the estate.'

Before either could react, the drawing room door opened once again and a footman announced the arrival of the Duke of Atholl. In strode the master of the house, fuming at the ears. His face had turned that ruddy complexion peculiar to men who indulge to excess in whisky or port wine, and his eyes, Victoria was alarmed to notice, bulged with fury. The overall impression was that of a bristling bear, cornered and ready to fight. Behind this vision trailed two soldiers and the old forester, Thomas, holding his cap in one hand and slicking down his greasy hair with the other.

'Ma'am,' the Duke began, then hesitated and made a little bow. Victoria noted that he was taking great pains to keep his expression under control.

'Good morning,' she said amiably. 'Would you be good enough to come back in a quarter of an hour? I shall require a vehicle and some men to accompany me on a drive down Glen Tilt.'

'I am afraid I must protest.'

'And why is that, Murray?'

'This man is not who he says he is!' He pointed at Balfour and scowled so that the tufts of his eyebrows met in the middle like opposing armies. 'Whatever lies he has told you, I beg you not to heed them. By God, I will not have him in my house. He is one of the blackguards who has attacked me twice now and trespassed on my reserve.'

Balfour jumped to his feet and faced up to the Duke. Victoria was surprised to see that the academic-turned-adventurer was in fact taller than Murray by a not inconsiderable amount; nevertheless, the Duke had a sword sheathed at his belt and two dangerous-looking Atholl Highlanders standing to attention. She prayed it would not come to a fight here in the drawing room.

If the Duke had seemed angry, Professor Balfour was apoplectic.

'This really is more than I can take. You might be the landowner, sir, and a powerful man, but I will have none of it, do you hear? I have done nothing but assert my right to travel an ancient pass, and moreover I am a member of the Royal household and an influential fellow in my own way. You shall feel the full weight of the law for this!'

Suddenly the Duke seemed to lose his resolve. He took a step back and blinked as if seeing Balfour for the first time; for, in truth, he no longer looked like a dishevelled poacher. He stood tall, hands folded on his breast, nostrils flared, chin jutting out confidently, eyes blazing.

'I can assure you that this man is indeed John Balfour,' Victoria added. She had no desire to get involved in this squabble, but felt obliged to weigh in on behalf of the man she had wronged last night.

Balfour did not break his stare with the Duke. 'And furthermore, the men currently being chased north by Prince Albert and your men are colleagues of mine from the University of Edinburgh. What do you say to that?'

'I say that they have no business on my land, and that I am well within my rights to arrest trespassers. One of those men is a dangerous criminal who has a personal dispute with me.'

Victoria grew weary of this argument. *This is supposed to be a family holiday. It feels more like a shouting match in the House of Lords.* She sighed loudly and stood up, smoothing down the front of her dress with both hands.

The Duke wisely took this as a sign to stop talking, and stood there looking frightened, like a rabbit caught in a snare.

All present paused and watched the Queen, awaiting her judgement. Only Mrs Forbes dared look at her directly, and when Victoria saw that spark of hope in her eyes she knew she was taking the right course of action. She felt a strong thread of kinship with this woman who had been left behind to look after the children while her husband had gone off adventuring by himself. Besides, whether or not the scientists had been right to enter the Duke's reserve without permission, men of society did not deserve such barbaric treatment. Such things were not to be endured in her kingdom.

'Murray, you will arrange for a vehicle, ponies, and a dependable guide. I shall travel with Isaac and go in search of my dear Albert. It will do me good to see some of the countryside.'

The Duke exhaled deeply. His face was sweating. 'Ma'am, again I must strongly protest. Criminals must be apprehended, not reprieved.'

She raised her voice. The time for calm discourse was over.

'And again I must remind you that I am your sovereign and you will obey me! Must I repeat every command I give? Did you not promise me that I would be mistress of this house for the duration of my visit? I wish to travel north and you will do everything in your power to ease my journey!'

'At least allow me to accompany you.'

'I forbid it.' She smiled at Balfour, calm once again. 'Instead, you are to provide transport for this gentleman back to Edinburgh, if he is agreeable. Now shake hands like good fellows.'

The Duke did not move.

'I insist,' she added.

The belligerents faced each other awkwardly. The Duke looked so ill at ease that for a moment Victoria thought he might actually faint; Balfour, on the other hand, had the look of a man who had just won a great battle. Reluctantly, they shook hands.

Balfour turned and bowed deeply to the Queen. 'I am in your debt. The University will not forget this kindness.'

'Go with our blessing, Professor. Make the gardens in Edinburgh beautiful for our next visit.'

Without another word, the Duke withdrew with his Highlanders. Balfour followed shortly afterwards, leaving Victoria and Mrs Forbes alone in the drawing room. The young lady shrank back into her chair as if overpowered now that the attention of the Queen was focused on her alone.

Nevertheless, she found the courage to look into Victoria's eyes and ask a question.

'Will you let me come with you, Ma'am?'

'In your condition? I will not hear of it.'

'But I simply must go. What if the illness has weakened his constitution?'

'Then we shall take the best care of him.' Victoria reached out and took the poor woman's hand in her own. It felt cold and did not respond to her touch. 'I understand how worried you must be. I promise that I shall do everything I can to help your husband.'

'Thank you,' Mrs Forbes whispered.

'Some good must come out of this regrettable incident.' Victoria smiled at her again. 'Now go back to your children and wait for my message. Thank you for coming to see me about this, my dear.'

When Mrs Forbes had gone, Victoria called for her maid and dictated a list of items that must be packed in preparation for the journey. As she gathered her children about her and explained that she would be going on a drive into the country to search for their father, she reflected that this holiday was proving to be quite an adventure after all.

* * *

Alec McAdie scanned Glen Geusachan through his telescope, searching with increasing desperation for the beast they had hunted for so long. After ten minutes of fruitless search he was forced to give up. Damh-mor was not there. Although herds of lesser deer walked the flat and boggy miles of the glen below, no sign of the great hart could be discerned.

Now he had to decide what to do.

Prince Albert looked haggard after the night in the open. Never the most robust of men, it was said he had suffered from frequent illness as a youngster and, despite his zeal for the outdoor life, his health was fragile. Yesterday's run up the flanks of Beinn Bhrotain would have been enough to tire out a fit man, but the Prince had clearly suffered from the experience. A night out of doors had not helped matters. Albert was used to spending his nights on the hunt in the comfortable quarters of a forest lodge.

Now he was peevish and snapped at the foresters.

'Do you mean to say we have no facility for brewing coffee? Can we not make a fire?'

Duncan perched atop the cairn of Monadh Mor, squinting into the sunshine and counting off the distant peaks on the horizon. The night in the open had not affected him in the slightest; McAdie knew that, when his watch was over, Duncan had fallen asleep the moment he had laid down his head, and had not wasted a moment of his resting hours. Now he was refreshed and ready for another day of pursuit. McAdie felt pride in that fact, at least. He had not completely failed to train his son in the ways of the estate forester.

'Wo ist mein Hirsch?'

Prince Albert stood up and faced McAdie, nostrils flaring, thinning hair greasy and uncombed. McAdie perceived that today would be his last chance to bring Albert within shooting range of the hart.

He took off his cap and bowed his head respectfully. 'He'll be fair donnered af'er the chase, sir. Happen he has gone to soil ... elsewhere.'

'Speak plainly, man! Can you or can you not bring me my hart?'

'Aye, it can be done. I ... I beg your forgiveness. I was mistook. All my instincts told me he would go to soil in the glen below, but he isnae there.'

Duncan jumped from his perch and began checking over the pony's saddle. A strange look had come over the lad's face and McAdie realised at once that Duncan knew why the hart was not to be found.

He grabbed his son by the scruff of the neck and hauled him in front of the Prince. Duncan protested but went limp the moment he fell under Albert's disapproving frown.

'D'ye have something to tell us, laddie?' McAdie demanded. 'Where is the beast?'

'He's gone. We'll ne'er catch him now.'

'Gone where?'

'Forbes and his companion camped below Bod an Deamhain last night. They scared him off.' Duncan's expression grew wretched. 'He'll have run north, and with the others on his tail he'll nae stop running.'

McAdie took a moment to comprehend what his son was telling him. How could Duncan possibly know this?

Before he could speak, Prince Albert intervened. He made a motion for McAdie to release his son.

'Now then,' Prince Albert said in a kindly manner, his anger forgotten. 'I think it is easy to understand what has occurred here, is it not? Let us examine the facts. When we came across the intruders at the Tarf water, they were in two groups. Duncan held them at bay from the rocks … and yet now we discover that he not only knows the name of one of these poachers, he is also privy to their plans!'

McAdie did not follow the Prince's reasoning, but Duncan stood his ground and said nothing.

'It is clear to me that your son was paid to guide one of these men through the estate from Pitlochry,' Albert continued, 'and that at the ford this "Forbes" met with accomplices who were perhaps unknown to Duncan. Caught between duty and greed, he decided to defend the borders of his land. Am I correct?'

Duncan remained silent. McAdie touched his son's arm, and he turned to look at his father, expression defiant. All of a sudden McAdie realised that Duncan had grown up and was slipping out of his control. Perhaps he was his own man after all ... and yet he could not comprehend this betrayal of the estate, of his family, of everything Duncan had been brought up to believe and hold close to his heart.

'Is this true?'

'Aye, and what if it is? You may have wasted your life serving a master who will never reward your efforts, but I'll not do the same!'

That cut McAdie to the core. How could he be so selfish?

'I hope you know what you've done to our family.'

'Can ye not understand I had to do something for *me?* All my life I've served *you* and his lordship!'

Despite his bold words, McAdie saw that his son looked truly wretched.

Albert stepped between the two men, gently holding them apart. 'Look at me, McAdie.'

Reluctantly, he complied.

'Tell me the truth. Your master has threatened you with eviction if you fail to please me, is that correct?'

McAdie nodded mutely.

'And in order to perform this task you require the loyalty of your son. I do not blame the boy; he is young, and only wished to make the most of an opportunity.' Albert smiled at Duncan. 'I have observed that life in the Highlands is hard at the present time. It is wrong of me to put such pressure on you. Now that I know, it is my duty to help.'

McAdie opened his mouth to reply, but found his words had dried up. 'I'm afeart I may have lost your hart,' he managed at length.

Albert rubbed his hands together and chuckled. He no longer seemed tired; now he was animated and full of vigour, ready for another day on the hill. 'I am a sportsman, McAdie. A challenge does not deter me.'

Duncan looked at the Prince boldly. 'Begging your pardon, but you're wrong about one thing.'

'And what might that be?' Albert said.

'Forbes ne'er paid me a penny.'

'Then we must bring him to account.' Albert stroked his moustache. 'You are loyal servants, both of you, and you have impressed me with your hardiness and knowledge of the land. No more royal commands; we will treat one another as fellows, in good faith. If you help me find my hart, I will do all in my power to help you both. What do you say to that?'

McAdie looked at his son, who returned the glance. In Duncan's eyes he saw conflicting feelings: the desire to break away—that much was now obvious—mixed with the loyalty for home and estate that McAdie had tried so hard to instil in his son.

Duncan looked back at Prince Albert. 'Aye, cannae say fairer than that.'

* * *

By the time Forbes had led the horse into the grand amphitheatre of Bràigh Riabhach, he was once again starting to feel the effects of his illness. That final league, traversing rough hillside with no trace of a path underfoot, had tried his strength and his patience. How many times, he asked himself, had Carr sat comfortably in his saddle while Forbes probed the ground ahead for potholes and bogs?

Carr was at once a benefit and a burden to his expedition. Forbes would not like to journey into such a remote place alone, and yet in truth he would have chosen a steadier companion.

'Aha! Another burn ... let's see if the horse can clear it!'

Carr would spur his tiring mount to a trot and then take a flying leap over some torrent, guarded by rocks on the far bank. The consequences of their horse breaking her leg at this point in the journey were beyond imagining, so after the second of these little stunts Forbes confiscated the whisky and ordered his student to behave more in a more sober manner.

The first view of the Garbh-choire icefields put an end to all such games.

'At last,' Forbes breathed as he leaned against his staff and surveyed the dazzling jewels of the Cairngorms.

The bulk of Bràigh Riabhach was scooped out on the east side to form a colossal amphitheatre over a mile across. Perhaps at some point in antiquity it had been a volcano, or maybe the void was entirely the product of glaciation. Forbes would not know for certain until he had completed his survey. This valley delved into the heart of the mountain and was carved into several individual corries, guarded by a fringe of cliffs and each harbouring a secret reservoir of snow and ice. High to their left, a sharp ridge, flecked with snow here and there, led up to yet another nameless and unexplored pinnacle. Forbes had seen similar geological formations in the Alps. He had to pinch himself and recall to mind the fact that this was Scotland, his own native land.

How wondrous it is, he thought, *that such remarkable places should exist mere days from my own beloved Edinburgh.*

A little cloud had begun to form in the amphitheatre, well below the level of the clifftops, but he could easily see that the icefields were both extensive and seamed with innumerable crevasses. Only a closer inspection would determine whether or not these icefields were truly glacial in nature. If so, then the natural history of Scotland would be altered forever and once again the name of Forbes would be at the forefront of glaciology. How sweet would be such a triumph!

'You are grinning like a schoolboy with a tin train,' Carr observed. He sounded a little more sober now.

'I am at my happiest, my boy. This is what I was put on this earth to do.'

'Then let's get going, shall we?'

They proceeded into the corrie. Something moved up on the hillside to the left, on the other side of the torrent coming down from the snouts of the icefields, and a small landslide of scree echoed around that silent place.

* * *

The favourable weather lasted no longer than half a day.

Duncan sweated at the rear of the hunting party as they struggled up the southern flanks of yet another mountain. He had no clear idea where they were. For a few hours after dawn the sun had blazed down on them as it climbed into the heavens, and Duncan had tramped upwards, tormented by the heat, swatting midges out of his eyes and following the pony as she picked the most efficient path through the rocks. They had not lingered at the waterlogged *bealach* between the two mountains, for such places were blighted by a miasma of bad air that was known to cause disease.

The wind began to pick up after an hour, and by noon a veil of high cloud had completely obscured the sun. The humidity of their ascent soon turned to a dangerous chill. Every man in the party wore clothing dampened by the sweat of his exertion, and now the north wind stole body heat from them with every step.

Albert plodded grimly at his side. He hadn't spoken for an hour or more. Duncan wondered what thoughts might be passing through the mind of the Prince in this wild and remote place. Did he miss his wife and family? Was he bent purely on his single-minded pursuit of the prize, or did his thoughts return to weighty matters of politics and state?

Suddenly they emerged at the most savage and breathtaking location Duncan had ever seen in these mountains.

They had been following a burn uphill for a while now. The waters were often hidden beneath masses of old snow as they flowed down a furrow in the mountain. The hunters trod cautiously over this sugary carapace, and Duncan followed his father's footsteps, wary of concealed voids. Sometimes he could hear the water gurgling and foaming below his feet. The surface was so dirty and blown-over with grass and dust that it hardly looked like snow at all, but resembled the rocks to each side: a desolate expanse of grey, pock-marked and rippled like sand on a beach.

McAdie led their party to the source of this burn: a *bealach* between two mountain peaks. The wind blasted shreds of freezing mist through the notch, and in the gale Duncan could smell an imminent blizzard. An ache of foreboding settled in his bones as he approached that fearful place.

A boiling confusion of cloud hid the landscape here and there, first obscuring it completely then revealing it for a dazzling moment before covering it up once again. Duncan had never climbed this high before. To his mind this notch in the mountains was the very gateway into the hell belonging to the Bodach: a world forbidden to men, a kingdom of monsters and savage forces, of avalanches and death.

He raised a hand before his eyes to shield them from the terrible wind. Ahead, he could see no distinction between the snow on which he stood and the churning white of the sky. The ground trembled and groaned beneath his shoes. He raised his eyes to the mountain peak on the right: a vertical cliff, monstrous to his eyes, fringed by dripping icicles that reached down like claws into the abyss beneath.

His father stood on a rock, leaning over the edge, trying to penetrate the veil of cloud which filled the amphitheatre below. Duncan flailed through the snow in his direction.

'Where are we?'

'Stay back!' McAdie warned. 'There's a *barraman* here. I cannae see the edge.'

Barraman: an overhanging ledge of snow, poised to fall into the depths and kill any who stand upon it. Such evil traps were constructed by the Bodach and had claimed many a victim over the years.

Duncan felt the first flakes of snow whipping past his face, carried on the strengthening northerly. August snow was common in the high mountains, but today, after such a fine sunrise, it was an evil omen.

'We must climb down there.' McAdie pointed into the whirling darkness beneath them.

Albert struggled to his feet. 'Down there? Are you mad?'

'If the hart wasnae in Glen Geusachan he'll be in Garbh-coire for sure. This is our route down.'

McAdie took a step forward, sinking up to his ankles in the snow; then another step, and another, probing the ground ahead with the stock of his rifle. The fury of cloud blasting over the ridge obscured his outline so that he became little more than a wraith in a matter of seconds.

The landscape devoured him. Duncan turned to Albert, quaking inside but determined to make an outward show of confidence.

'You heard my father. No time for resting until we're in the corrie below.'

Albert nodded. The snow was beginning to stick to his moustache and he shivered in the cold. For a moment Duncan thought he detected fear in the great man's expression, but with a stoic smile Albert banished his doubts.

'I trust you. Lead the way.'

Duncan followed his father's footsteps to the edge of the abyss.

The wind increased with every step he took, grasping at his sleeves, tearing at his face with pellets of ice, striving to push him back into the mortal world. The snow sapped the warmth from his feet and made it harder to ignore the fatigue which had built up over days of hard work and poor rest. Such conditions killed men regularly, and in truth Duncan was mortally afraid, for they were entering the realm of the mountain spirits where the boundary between life and death was as narrow as a thread.

A man is an atom here. We do not belong, and we survive only by the grace of fate.

A rotten fissure gaped in the snow at his feet. Clogged with debris blown in from the corrie beneath, natural forces had sculpted it into the most fantastic shapes imaginable: a frozen morass of twisted crests and sinkholes, cracks and waves. He stepped over this barrier with care.

Beyond it, his father had kicked a trench in the overhanging lip of snow. Snowflakes blasted through this gap into Duncan's face, momentarily blinding him. Footsteps led down a slope of unremitting steepness on the other side: a clean sweep of a hundred yards, perhaps more, although much of the descent was hidden in the murk. He could see his father descending on all fours some way beneath, facing into the slope.

He turned back to address Albert. The Prince was coated in driven snow from his boots to the crown of his head, and he shielded his eyes with a hand as he staggered in the relentless wind.

'Mind how ye go, sir,' Duncan shouted at him. 'It's awful steep.'

'The pony will never make it down here! This is madness!'

'Trust her! She's a better climber than any of us.'

The mountain roared as Duncan began his descent, and in that roar he heard the unearthly cry of the Bodach.

* * *

Forbes looked out over the surface of what may or may not be Scotland's last glacier. To his irritation, bad weather had come in rapidly and destroyed any chance of making an overall observation until it cleared again. In the past when surveying glaciers he had climbed to some high point and drawn out a map of the terrain before placing his marker flags.

Now a freezing wind blew over the surface of the ice and began filling in the holes and crevasses with a fine layer of new snow. It melted almost as soon as it fell, but Forbes was reminded of days on the glacier above Chamouni in which the temperature had dropped from eighty degrees to below forty in a matter of a few hours. Massing ranks of cloud hid the clifftops far above.

He walked a few paces. The snow was soft and saturated with water. It felt granular and sugary between his fingers, and melted in seconds to leave grit, stalks of grass, and other flecks of matter behind. On a larger scale, debris blackened the surface of the snow in great bands that seemed to flow downhill from the crevasses above.

Cracks seamed this uneven surface. Some were only a few feet wide and no broader than a man's hand, while others were gaping slots capable of devouring a horse. Such crevasses were common in the mountains of the Alps, and a less experienced man would have proclaimed them evidence enough that this mass of snow was indeed a glacier; however, Forbes was not so easily convinced. He had seen semi-permanent snow patches in Norway which looked identical.

The distinction between a snow patch and a glacier was a minor but critical one. Only a true glacier flowed downhill and remained permanent throughout the years. *Only a true Scottish glacier,* he thought, *will bring my name back to the forefront of my field and remove the taint of Agassiz.*

The headache had returned, pounding away at the base of his skull and accompanied by a swaying nausea in his abdomen. He ignored it as best he could, although from time to time he was forced to lean against his staff and close his eyes in an effort to rally his defences.

I am here at last! I'll be damned if my own weakness will prevent me from carrying out this survey.

Carr crouched on a rock by the side of the ice, huddled up in his cloak and throwing pebbles into a pool. A tired look had come over him, and from time to time he looked up at the menacing cliffs and shivered. Forbes wondered if the shine of this adventure was starting to wear off for his student now that they had reached their destination.

'So what now, Professor?'

'Now I begin my survey.'

'Any way I can assist?'

'Stay out of mischief!' He smiled at Carr's aggrieved expression. 'All right, if you really want to be useful you can make some markers. Tear your spare shirt into strips and tie them to stones. I'll dye them red later.'

While his student was busy, Forbes took out his pocket book and scrawled a few notes with a stub of pencil.

Glacial(?) mass approximately 400 yards broad in east corrie of B. Riabhach

Surface soft summer snow. No bare ice in evidence

Wide rimaye at base of cliffs. Other crevasses may be glide cracks.

Full survey required to determine movement, if any"

A blast of wind cut through the damp fabric of his coat, and he shivered. *What I wouldn't give for a hearty roast dinner.* He had eaten nothing but vegetable stew and thin porridge for days now, and the meagre diet was sapping his reserves.

He heard a bang and a splash behind him, followed by a shout from his student.

'Damn!'

Forbes spun around to see that Carr had toppled from his boulder and now struggled in the pool at the edge of the snowpack, leg twisted under him, a startled expression on his face. He flailed with his arms, grasping for a tuft of grass with which to haul himself out of the freezing water.

'Help me!'

'You foolish boy.' He stepped forward to offer a hand, but felt unsteady as he braced himself against Carr's weight. 'Don't you know how dangerous it is to get wet through in cold weather? You had better change right away.'

'But I have torn up my shirt. Anyhow, I'm quite warm.'

Carr crouched by the edge of the pool, shivering and massaging the side of his injured foot. His eyes were unfocused and he shook his head once or twice as if to unclog his faculties.

A suspicion grew in Forbes' mind.

'Have you been drinking again?'

Carr staggered to his feet and shook himself like a dog, showering Forbes in droplets. 'What if I have? My foot hurts like the devil and we have no shelter! A man must have something to keep warm.'

His plaintive words were at odds with the brazen image he tried so hard to project. The reality, of course, was that Carr was a very young fellow who was desperate to impress. Beneath the bravado he was far from home, in pain, and most likely frightened.

Forbes took off his hat and ran a hand through his hair. *Am I selfish? Have I paid no attention to the needs of my companion?* On the other hand, Carr had studied the methods of his master, and ought to know what hardship a glacier survey entailed. He spoke of adventure, but did he not realise that true adventure was nothing but cold and fatigue, labour and danger in a place far from home?

'I really cannot understand your behaviour. Think of the opportunity! This could be the making of my career.'

'Your career was made long ago. You just don't appreciate what you have.'

Forbes didn't know what to say to that. He had a suspicion that his wife might agree. Angry with Carr for pointing out another of his weaknesses, he turned away and focused on the job he had come here to do.

I shall place five markers on the ice and triangulate their positions from fixed points on the corrie rim. A clear day to survey the clifftops ought to do it, plus three days of observations, and two days to ride back to Blair...

'How much food do we have?' he thought out loud.

'Look for yourself.'

He didn't care for Carr's surly tone, but decided not to press the matter. He rifled through the saddlebags, pulling out rolled blankets, the bottle of red dye he used for colouring glacier markers, and a spare pair of breeches before he came to the sack of food.

It felt much lighter than he had expected. He undid the knot and looked inside. It contained only a sack of oatmeal weighing a few pounds, a packet of iron-hard ship's biscuits (which Forbes had no intention of ever eating again unless he had no other choice), and a rotten potato.

'Would you care to explain,' he said, brandishing the potato in Carr's direction, 'how we are meant to survive for five or six days on this?'

Carr struggled to his feet and grabbed Forbes' staff, discarded on the snow, to use as a crutch. He hobbled in the direction of the saddlebags. That handsome face which had made the ladies of Edinburgh swoon was now contorted into a scowl of discontent. He snatched the food sack and returned it to the saddlebag.

'Five or six days! I thought your survey would take a day at most.'

'But you have read my book. My survey of the Mer de Glace took weeks.'

'That was the Alps. This is a bloody stupid little snow patch on a Scottish hill.'

'You are drunk, so I shall ignore that remark.'

'Clearly I am not drunk enough. I came out here for one last adventure before I am forced to accept reality, not a lengthy scientific endeavour!' He sat down unsteadily on a rock and cradled his head in his hands. 'What a bloody mess. You'd be better off without me, I can see that now.'

So there is something wrong. Forbes had wondered, more than once, if there was some fact Carr had concealed from him—perhaps something that might explain his behaviour.

'Tell me what is troubling you. Perhaps I can help.' He paused, feeling awkward. 'I've never been very good with this sort of thing, you know—counselling my students—but we're friends, are we not? You can talk to me, my boy.'

Carr remained silent and motionless for a long moment, and then a shudder passed through him as if he suffered from some mortal illness.

'You are the last man in the world who would understand. You have no tolerance for human weaknesses; you care only for ice and rocks.' With that he wrapped his cloak around his shoulders and lapsed into brooding, refusing any further communication.

Forbes decided to give up. Carr was obviously not going to tell him anything until it suited him. Although he knew he was being unkind, Forbes was furious with the boy and resolved to let him stew in his misery for a few hours. He felt like sermonising about the value of perseverance and sobriety but in the end held his tongue.

'Give me back my staff. If you are cold, build a shelter while I'm away.'

Forbes stuffed the glacier markers and red dye into his knapsack, taking care not to damage his scientific instruments, and struck off alone into the cloud and the whirling snowflakes.

* * *

Duncan was the first man in the hunting party to discover evidence of the hart in An Garbh-choire. He was surprised that his father had not noticed the spoor, for usually he had a superhuman ability to gauge the age, weight, sex, and running direction of a deer from the merest trace.

This time it was the imprint of a stag's hoof, pressed lightly into the fine white sand that filled up the gaps between the rocks and the bare patches of ground where heather had not taken root. He reached down to touch the edge of the print.

'Father!'

McAdie doubled back and approached Duncan's position at a crouched run, carrying his gun lightly in one hand and his telescope in the other. He squinted down at the footprint through his bushy eyebrows and actually smiled.

'He's nae far away, laddie. We'll catch him yet.'

At his father's order, the party dropped down to a crawl. This far up the mountain the heather grew more sparsely and did not form the thickets that swamped the lower flanks; consequently it was easier to move unhindered while flat on one's front, but keeping out of sight was more difficult. Duncan had wrapped a rag of oilcloth around the lock of his rifle to protect it against the damp. After letting Floraidh loose to graze, he began the painstaking crawl over the stones and boggy ground that filled the bottom of An Garbh-choire. A mountain hare watched them with twitching nose.

An hour passed, and another. They sighted a deer high on the side of Sgor an Lochain Uaine, but it was not the beast they sought. Ever patient, methodical, and tireless, McAdie led them gradually uphill, following a trajectory to one side of where he knew the hart would be concealed amongst the hillocks of the burn.

Finally the hours of careful manoeuvring paid off. McAdie raised his hand to indicate that their target had been sighted.

Cloud swirled and smoked over a spur of land, beyond which awaited a depthless expanse of white. They had come to the *eigh-shruth*: the ancient ice that never dies. In the gloom it possessed neither radiance nor any discernible form, merely an absence of colour and texture, a void in the substance of the mountain.

Something moved between the ice and the driving sleet. Visible only by its silhouette, a hart—*the* hart—stepped out from behind a boulder and stood calmly in the centre of their field of vision, perhaps thirty yards distant.

Had it seen them? Was this coincidence, or had it brought them to this place?

He glanced at Albert. The Prince was wound up like an eight-day clock, his breathing ragged, every atom of his attention focused on the shadow of the stag he had hunted for so long.

'Tell me what to do, McAdie!'

If possible, Duncan's father was even more animated than Albert. For the first time in years he actually looked happy: the thrill of the hunt was with him, his eyes were alight with fervour instead of cynicism, and for a moment Duncan forgot that he wanted to escape this life.

'Ye'll have but one shot. Make it count, aye?'

The hunters lay side by side on top of a little rise. Albert loaded his rifle, an awkward manoeuvre in his prone position, but after a few minutes raised it to his shoulder and sighted along the barrel.

'Compensate for the wind,' McAdie whispered. 'Take your time.'

Albert reached up with his right hand and pulled back the hammer, then settled into his aim. Duncan held his breath as if it was him about to pull the trigger and not the Prince. Every member of the party lay absolutely still and silent, eyes trained on the stag, praying for the outcome they had anticipated these past two days. It all depended on their client now. The most skilled forester in the land could not affect the course of a rifle ball.

Have a good death, Damh-mor, Duncan thought, *and I hope the Bodach forgives us for this.*

The hart twitched his ears and took a step forward. The graceful beast had not the slightest notion that he was about to die.

Albert's rifle barked. The report echoed around the amphitheatre of An Garbh-choire, and when the smoke blew away Duncan peered into the mist, looking for any trace of their fallen target.

'Did I hit him?'

There! The hart bounded from rock to rock, escaping deeper into the corrie. McAdie muttered a curse and brought his own rifle to bear, firing at the swiftly departing animal.

The second shot also missed. Damh-mor disappeared into the impenetrable white.

Nobody spoke.

Albert was the first to move. He sat upright, brushed a little of the mud from his coat, and set his rifle carefully down on the ground. He looked shaken, as if he could not quite believe that he had missed his shot after all this time.

'McAdie, would you be good enough to give me a little whisky?'

McAdie handed him the flask with a shaking hand. Their eyes met for an instant before the forester looked away, concealing his disappointment and frustration.

'A good try, sir.'

Albert took a slug of whisky and handed back the flask. 'Don't try to flatter me. It was a poor shot.'

As Albert spoke, Duncan became aware of a change in the atmosphere about them. It started with a gathering of the clouds above their head: a swirling blackness that poured sleet and snow down on them in merciless torrents. The wind tore at their clothes and for a few moments the hunters clung to each other, bewildered by the sudden ferocity of the storm.

Lightning stabbed down out of the darkness—once! twice!—followed by a rumbling explosion that shook the mountain to its core.

Duncan closed his eyes. Twin white streaks were left imprinted on the field of his vision. He felt his whole body shaking, and only at this point did he truly comprehend the crime they had committed. How could they possibly expect to trespass on the Bodach's territory, to hunt his game, and avoid punishment?

'We have to get away from here,' he shouted at the others. 'The Bodach will kill us if we stay!'

His father turned to look at him. The hope had gone from his eyes, and all thanks to a missed rifle shot. He may not believe in the Bodach but he knew when he was beaten.

McAdie gave a weary sigh. 'Aye, my boy's right. We should leave now while we can.'

Albert looked from man to man. 'And I say we shall *not* leave! By God, I thought you were outdoorsmen. What of our agreement? The hart is still out there and I'll be damned if I'm going to turn away without my prize after all this time!'

'But the storm—!'

'We build a shelter and wait until it clears. You have proven you have what it takes. Pray give me a chance to do the same.'

Albert and McAdie glared at each other. The old forester had set aside his habitual deference now that he perceived his battle had been lost. Albert, with whom Duncan had spoken on such familiar terms yesterday, once again looked every inch the man of power he really was: indignant, immovable, nostrils flared and eyes blazing. The long miles and the weather had reduced them all to the same miserable physical condition, but it was clear to Duncan that the Prince would not give up his cause.

'I'll not risk our lives, sir,' McAdie persisted. 'Not for the sake of a stag.'

'Not even for the promise I made to you? I shall help you both, that I swear, but in exchange I ask for one more day.'

McAdie grumbled under his breath. Duncan knew what would be going through his mind: a complex balancing up of all factors a forester must consider on the mountain.

'One day, aye?'

'One day. If I miss again then I shall consider myself fairly beaten.'

McAdie closed his eyes and shook his head. He looked so very tired. Duncan had become accustomed to associating feelings of frustration and resentment with his father, but now he felt ashamed for all his selfish impulses. So much depended on this hunt and the notion of giving up was a hard one to bear.

'All right, then,' McAdie said finally. 'Against my better judgement this may be, but ye deserve a second chance—cannae say fairer than that.'

They shook hands, each holding onto his cap against the wind, and straightaway set about the task of building a wall to protect themselves from the driving snow.

"EIGHT FATHOMS AND SOLID GROUND"

CHAPTER VI
THE BODACH

FORBES TOOK ANOTHER STEP and leaned against his staff, taking deep, ragged breaths. From a mild twinge yesterday afternoon the pain in his head had steadily worsened, and now it hammered away on the inside of his skull like a sledgehammer against marble. He was barely able to concentrate on the task of placing glacier markers. The symptoms had not been this bad for over a year, and he knew if his wife were here she would insist upon an immediate return to Edinburgh and a consultation with his physician.

Slowly, he opened his eyes and lifted his head to look into the whirlpool of snow and storm that surrounded him.

He had succeeded in climbing to the highest point on the "glacier": the gaping crevasse which divided the bulk of the ice from the mountain itself. Above his head, icicles clung to an undercut shelf of rock, and beyond that, near-vertical slabs reached up into the heavens. A continuous stream of fine snow poured down this slab and over his body, somehow finding the back of his neck despite his wide-brimmed hat (which he was constantly in fear of losing to the wind) and neckcloth.

He probed the lip of the crevasse with his staff. A chunk of snow broke away and burst into mush on the far wall, which was bare rock, slick with water. With numb fingers he retrieved the plumbline from his pocket and lowered it into the depths.

One fathom. Two fathoms. Three fathoms .... five ... eight fathoms and solid ground.

He had expected the crevasse to be deeper. It certainly looked wide enough; he was unable to reach the far wall with an outstretched arm, although he did not dare step too close to the crumbling edge. For a moment he entertained the awful thought of what would happen to him if he fell down there, eight fathoms down to a slow grave sandwiched between the rock of the mountain and the layers of ice he had devoted his life to studying. His knees felt weak and he took a step back from the chasm.

Focus! Be the master of your body, not its slave.

He coiled his plumbline and began a careful descent of the snowslope. The angle was dangerous here—his clinometer put it at 43 degrees, although it felt steeper—and he took care to kick steps with the heel of his boot, and not move down until he was certain the platform would bear his weight without collapsing. Sometimes he had to bring the point of his staff into action and chip away at the solid ice just beneath the surface. It was hard work, but he had done it many times before in the old days.

Nevertheless, the effort was a strain, and he wished he had a Swiss guide armed with hatchet and rope.

He had descended no more than ten yards before a peculiar sensation came over him. His heart palpitated, pins and needles rushed to the palms of his hands and the pit of his stomach, and the roar of the storm faded in his ears. He could see the pulse of his own heartbeat. His body began to shake, and he felt a terrible fear that he was about to suffer some apoplexy and die where he stood. Strangely, the headache had disappeared.

He gulped in breath after breath. *I am the master of my body*. He tried to fight the panic with the force of his will.

The corrie howled around him, an uncaring cauldron of cold and pain, suffused with an eerie glow that shone down from above. As his vision began to fade he saw a spectre approaching through the mist: a fearful shadow, black against blinding white, surrounded by a halo that—to his terrified mind—signified the end of his time on this Earth.

His vision dissolved to black, and he felt nothing more.

* * *

Consciousness returned to James Forbes in the piecemeal fashion familiar to those awakening from exceptionally deep sleep.

At first he was aware only of textures, felt rather than seen: interlocking shapes and colours that pulsed and changed, first an array of tiny triangles, then something like a slick of oil on a pond, then shapes that defied all description. Fragments of dreams swam in and out of this mental substrate. Gradually he perceived less of his confused dreamworld and more of the tangible environment around him.

Consciousness returned.

He opened his eyes but could see nothing but white. The pain had spread from his head and stomach to the rest of his body, and his limbs were contorted beneath him, trapped between his own weight and the substance of the mountain. He blinked a few times in an effort to dispel the last of the grogginess.

He tried to sit up, but soon discovered that he was lying upside down on a steep slope about a hundred feet below the place where he had lost consciousness. The snow gave way beneath his body and he plunged another ten or fifteen feet, coming to rest in an ungainly sideways position a few feet from the edge of a gaping crevasse. Chunks of wet snow broke away from the lip and plunged into the darkness. Panic gripped him and he tried to dig his fingers into the slope and claw his way back up. Momentum was inexorable, however, and the snow exceptionally slippery. With every despairing movement he made, gravity sent him another inch down the slope.

He stopped struggling and looked up into the heavens. The cloud seemed less dense now. Sunlight smiled through here and there, but to Forbes this mountain had become a dreadful place, untouched by the grace of God. Perhaps there really was some malign presence here.

His attention returned to his predicament. The crack was deep but not wide, and the slope on the other side levelled out after a run of maybe fifty feet. To escape on either side was impossible unless he could gain a firm footstep. The laws of physics would permit only downward movement.

Then down I must go.

He judged that he could make the other side if he built up enough speed. Digging his left hand deep into the saturated snow pack, he inched himself around until he was facing downhill, more or less—and then he launched himself down the slope *en glissade.*

He only had a yard or two to gain momentum, but it was enough to propel him over the void. With a bump he hit the far bank and kept going. His legs burned with pain at the impact but it was too late to do anything about it now; he couldn't stop himself even if he wanted to, and the best he could hope to achieve was to keep a steady course.

Slush sprayed up on either side of his body as he accelerated. He cleared another crack with a bump, and veered left after striking a rock, hidden in a melted hollow in the surface. He wished he had his staff to control the descent, but, along with his knapsack and scientific instruments, it had been claimed by the mountain after his fall.

Gradually the slope levelled out. He halted near one of the markers he had placed a few hours ago: a splash of colour in an otherwise monochrome universe. His body had piled up a rampart of snow in front of him as he descended, like a snowplough, and now he found himself partially buried in the debris.

Now that he was past all immediate danger, Forbes realised just how cold he had become. All of his clothes were saturated to the skin with water. He shivered violently as he tried to stand up, and the intense cold made him feel even weaker. A gust of wind cut through him as easily as a scalpel and it took every ounce of his will not to collapse back down on the snow.

Both legs felt badly bruised and hurt to the touch but were not broken, thank God. His left knee would not bend more than a few degrees.

A persistent grogginess mired his mental faculties. He shook his head a few times in an attempt to dislodge the weakness, but if anything it only made him feel more unsteady.

Only after taking stock of how weak and battered he had become did Forbes truly realise that his survey of Bràigh Riabhach had to come to an end. Even if he had not suffered any injury, without his precious theodolite, compass, and clinometer he could do no work of value. He had failed.

So it has all been for nothing. I should have listened to my wife and stayed at Eastertyre.

The landscape swayed and swam before his eyes. He shook his head again.

Focus! I am alive and upright. My priority now is survival.

He had no accurate idea what o'clock it was, but he judged evening must be approaching fast. Death by exposure would follow soon enough. His only hope now was to join up with Carr and pray they could find enough fuel for a fire.

* * *

Victoria clasped her cloak to her shoulders and shivered. Another volley of snow and hail battered against her body, chilling her skin and sapping her spirits. She had been riding north for many hours now, had refused the chance of an overnight stay at Lochain Lodge—and all in the hope of finding Albert and bringing him back to the castle.

I should not have had to do this at all, she said to herself as she steered her pony around a rock in the middle of the path. *He ought to know that I expect him present at the castle on the morning of his birthday.*

Nevertheless, she tried not to think unkind thoughts about her husband. He had been quite taken with the legend of the mighty stag, and perhaps it was only natural that he should pursue it to the ends of the Earth if necessary. In truth, she had not expected the journey to take this long; her party had already travelled over twenty five miles, and still there was no sign of Albert or the gamekeepers. She had sent Isaac ahead to sniff out the trail, and was confident that the Jaeger would be able to find his master.

Like so many other places in Scotland, she associated the beautiful scenery of Glen Tilt with her dear Albert, with whom she had ridden through this glen on several occasions. To travel through such a sublime wilderness without him was in her opinion a shame. She made a deliberate point of not enjoying a moment of it until he was by her side again.

Old Thomas rode a little way ahead. He turned his pony and trotted back to draw level with Victoria, and she saw that, despite his hardiness, even he was suffering a little from the weather. His cap flopped over one eye and the high collar of his Inverness cape had gone soft from the damp; nevertheless, his eyes were bright as ever, and he had somehow succeeded in lighting his clay pipe, which smoked in the breeze.

'Begging your pardon, Ma'am, but when were ye thinking o' stopping for the night?'

'When I say so, Thomas,' she replied cheerfully, trying to mask her weariness. 'There must be hours of daylight left. Am I wrong?'

'No, not at all.' He scratched his bearded chin and gave a puzzled smile. 'We might make for one o' the shielings at the Chest of Dee. The weather—'

'I hope to find Albert and the others tonight. Is that clear? I don't intend to stop until my husband is safe. Isaac is bound to find the trail sooner or later. I don't know what your master has told you about my abilities as an outdoorswoman, but I can assure you that I am no stranger to perilous mountain voyages.'

Thomas did not look surprised, but then again in her experience Highland foresters rarely displayed that emotion. He merely shrugged, puffed on his pipe, and offered her a toothy smile.

'Aye, that I can see. Happen you'd make a good stalker, your Majesty.'

She laughed. 'I don't think so, but I thank you for the compliment.'

Thomas turned and rode on, and Victoria smiled to herself as she followed her guide along the rutted track into the desolation of the Mar Forest.

* * *

Upon reaching the stone by the pool at the edge of the snow, Forbes was dismayed to find that Ewan Carr was not there, and neither was the horse; only a pile of baggage remained, drifted over with snow, left in the lee of a crude stone wall.

Forbes staggered over to the bags, step by painful step. *Why is Carr not here? Where can he have gone?* He looked in all directions but could see nothing through the cloud and snow. Even the movement of turning his head and body was painful. He still felt dazed, and some submerged part of his consciousness was aware that his mind was not working as it should. Every thought was an effort. His body was inarticulate as a puppet, every movement wooden and clumsy.

Perhaps I hit my head…

With numb fingers he cleared a little snow from the saddlebag and unfastened the buckles, then reached inside. The first object he touched was a piece of paper. He pulled it into the light and examined it. His eyes focused, slowly, on the words.

> My dear Professor Forbes,
>
> Sorry to leave you like this—I feel beastly for it, & really my excuses are feeble, but you deserve an explanation. I pray these heartfelt & sober (!!) words will serve my purpose.
>
> The truth is that I am without a shilling. I own nothing but my clothes. Even the horse is stolen. There: I have admitted it at last.
>
> My father paid for my studies at the university, but he passed away six months ago. I tried my best to invest his fortune wisely but fell prey to the temptations of Edinburgh &, as you may have guessed, suffered substantial losses at the card table. My final defeat occurred one month ago when I

played against the Duke of Atholl, who is a member of my club.

In short he cleaned me out, but according to custom allowed me a chance to win back my money. I won the game—there are witnesses who will swear to it—but the villain refused to pay. He humiliated me in front of my friends and departed from the city, stopping only to make arrangements for the repossession of my family home.

I had a rash plan to confront the Duke in the wild & force him to return what is rightfully mine. Balfour is not to blame. I attached myself to his party & told him nothing of my motives, although he proved to be an ally when the Duke threatened us for trespassing. Shots were fired on both sides; that I think you have already surmised.

I have no notion of how to rescue anything from the wreck of my life, but I realise the time has come to stop drifting & do something rational for a change. You have shown me the wisdom of that! I must find the Duke & somehow convince him to give me what I am owed.

Now that I have made up my mind I cannot waste another minute. I know you will find it in your heart to forgive a wretch who has done nothing to deserve the many kindnesses you have shown him over the years. I leave you the blankets & what food remains.

I remain, sir, your loyal friend,

E.M.E. Carr

His first thought upon reading the letter was that Carr had lost his wits, or was perhaps still under the influence of liquor and playing a youthful prank. He struggled through the letter again. It sounded sober and sincere—unusually so on both counts.

How can it be that I was not aware of this?

Forbes now realised that he had been so consumed with his obsession, so wrapped up in the journey and the mountain at the end of it, that he had not spoken to Carr about his own life at all. He had not spared a single thought for Carr or why he might be spending his summer tramping over the Highlands instead of applying himself to the task of building a career. He had taken advantage of his old student, used him as a companion simply because he was afraid of travelling alone.

Now he was gone. Forbes folded the letter and placed it back in the saddlebag.

He looked up into the storm. The weather showed no signs of improvement; if anything, the wind had become more ferocious in the last hour, the snow more determined in its assaults on the crumbling fortress of his body. Every rock had a little prow of fresh snow built up behind it, sculpted by the wind and growing by the minute. The dirt bands on the ice were hidden now as the landscape turned a more pristine white. Every time Forbes looked down at the front of his coat he brushed away the crust of snow that had built up over the last few minutes.

Flake by flake, gust by gust, the weather was killing him.

He crouched by the low stone wall Carr had built. No higher than a man's knee, the meagre windbreak would not be enough to keep him alive, even if he piled himself high with blankets. Fortunately rocks were the one thing this barren place had in abundance. Perhaps if he improved the shelter and lit a fire he might survive until dawn.

And after that?

He could not permit himself the luxury of wasted thought. Exhausted he may be, but Forbes was a fighter at heart, and he set about his new task with as much energy as he could muster.

* * *

Duncan wondered if he was going mad. Did the others not see what he could see? Could they not hear the Bodach screaming on the wind?

The cloud above thickened as the light faded. Night could not be far away now. The snow came down more furiously with every passing hour, coating the landscape in a layer of slush that soaked everything it touched: a sticky, uncomfortable mess that melted just slowly enough to chill the hunters to the bone. When Duncan looked over the edge of the wall he saw shapes moving in the darkness. The fear had been building for hours and in the long silences between conversation he felt it gnawing at him, eroding his defences.

Albert, who had been snoozing, opened his eyes with a jolt and cried out something in German. He stared at Duncan with unfocused eyes and it took a moment for awareness to return.

'It's me, sir,' Duncan said, laying a hand on his shoulder to calm him. 'A bad dream, aye?'

'Perhaps. Is there any food?'

Duncan's father, who was keeping watch and had not moved in over half an hour, turned to look at the Prince. His craggy features dripped with water.

'The vittles are with the pony.'

'Well, I am hungry. Where is she?'

McAdie gestured out into the murk. He seemed inclined neither to engage in conversation nor go in search of Floraidh and the food. Albert looked so miserable and hungry that Duncan decided to ignore his own fears; their future, after all, might depend on Albert's good favour. Besides, he was hungry himself.

He picked up his rifle and checked the oilcloth was still in place, protecting his powder and shot. The full force of the wind hit him the moment he stood up.

'I'll go and find her. She'll nae have gone far.'

Albert smiled. 'God bless you, Duncan.'

The young ghillie left the safety of the shelter and struck out into the darkness. He knew only that Floraidh would have made her way downhill to better grazing and more sheltered ground.

What am I doing here? I should be in Edinburgh by now with a prosperous job and money in my pocket.

He dismissed the resentful thought. It had no place here. Such wishes were for idle evenings at Lochain Lodge, not for situations like this when he needed all of his energy to survive. Besides, his only true regret was that he had not helped Forbes when he should have done. Duncan had betrayed his trust and would regret that decision for a long time. Hopefully the ailing Professor had turned back before the storm had blown in.

Floraidh's tracks were not difficult to find. She had followed the fast flowing Allt a'Gharbh-choire by its south bank, and her passage was marked by tufts of black heather, shaken free of snow by the beast's limbs. He raised a hand to protect his eyes from the sleet and snow but could not see far downhill: a hundred yards at most, beyond which the land and sky merged into a swirling palette of grey.

'Floraidh!' he shouted, hoping his voice would carry far enough.

The mountain replied to his call. Lightning forked out of the sky, smiting a boulder a little way uphill. The blast knocked Duncan off his feet and for a few moments he cowered face down in the mud, hands over his ears, the noise of the storm silenced by an awful ringing that seemed to emanate from the base of his skull and consume all of his senses. He could feel sparks burning the back of his neck and when he finally summoned up the courage to open his eyes he saw that the boulder had been blasted to atoms by the explosion.

Merciful God protect me!

He felt unsteady when he stood up, and it took a minute for his hearing to recover completely. He continued to stagger downhill by the side of the burn. Now the fear had returned and he was unable to stop his body shivering in apprehension.

He could see something huge moving through the mist ahead.

Its shape could not be easily discerned in the poor lighting. Duncan hid behind a boulder and squinted into the distance to try and get a better view. It now appeared to him as the giant figure of a man, shadowy and indistinct, moving slowly and with a ponderous swaying motion. Duncan rubbed his eyes and looked again. It was hard to make anything out in this poor visibility. From time to time the spectre disappeared altogether, only to reappear moments later somewhere else.

Another lightning bolt flickered out of the heavens; more distantly this time, somewhere behind the spectre, which was suddenly illuminated by a halo of blinding light. The ground trembled under Duncan's feet. He had absolutely no doubt what the creature up ahead might be: it was the laird of these hills, the spectre he had feared all his life, and the one who had trapped them all in this terrible place.

He considered running back to the shelter and cowering there, waiting for whatever end the Bodach had planned for them all. He considered running off by himself into the storm and trying to find his way to safety. Neither course of action would solve his problems, and so Duncan came to an instinctive decision. He unwrapped the oilcloth from his rifle and rested the barrel on top of his boulder, sighting into the mist. Water dripped from the metalwork.

Could the Bodach even be killed? He had no idea. Like most of the important decisions he had made in his life, he acted purely on gut feeling.

The spectre moved again. It was closer now, but he felt more secure knowing he had some way of striking back. Duncan pulled back the lock and checked the cap was in place. His finger rested on the trigger. Just a few steps more…

Crack!

The rifle kicked back against his shoulder, and when the smoke cleared Duncan saw the ponderous shape lurch from side to side before dropping to the ground, immobile.

* * *

As he ran towards the site of his fallen adversary Duncan wondered what he would find when he got there. He had always believed that the Bodach could take almost any form, spectral or tangible. The stories said he could travel as a creature of air and vapour, as a monstrous hound, or as a man.

The shape on the ground shifted as he approached, prompting Duncan to tread more warily. He dropped to his knees and poured a charge of powder down the barrel, followed by a scrap of wadding and a ball. No time to load the rifle properly; he simply tapped the stock against the ground to seat the charge, applied another percussion cap, and raised the weapon. His hands no longer shook.

The fear had gone. He felt calm and detached, utterly focused.

He approached as his father had taught him, crawling no higher than a dog, taking care to stay downwind of the target. The barrel-chested shape on the ground thrashed and roared in pain.

To his surprise he heard a very human voice cry out nearby.

'You've killed my horse, you devil!'

A figure stood and faced him not five paces away. The man—for it was obviously a mortal human—raised a pistol and fired it at point blank range. The weapon sparked. Duncan closed his eyes and dropped flat, expecting to die before he hit the ground.

His heart thudded once, twice. The world spun above his head and Duncan waited for the searing pain to wash over him, but it did not come. After a moment he realised he had heard no gunshot.

The powder must be wet!

He raised the barrel of his rifle through the heather stalks and aimed it at the stranger's chest. It would be so easy to return fire and eliminate the threat, but in his heart Duncan knew that this figure was a poor wretch of a man, no spectre at all, and the shape slumped between two boulders a few paces away was the body of a dying horse.

Duncan lay motionless, frozen by indecision.

The man he had attacked limped forward a few steps. Young, perhaps not much older than Duncan himself, the traveller's eyes blazed in anger but there was something frail in the way he stood, as if the next gust of wind would knock him over. The stranger stopped and stared directly down the barrel of Duncan's rifle. His body trembled as if it were no more substantial than an autumn leaf—and yet his expression was one of shocked indignation.

When he laughed, the sound was cracked, tormented.

'Kill me, then! You people have done nothing but shoot at me since I first set foot in these hills. Finish it at last! I'd welcome it, and I know the Duke would be overjoyed. Wipe my mistakes clean!'

He threw his useless pistol to the ground. Duncan stood up and took a pace towards the poor man, who shivered violently and held his cloak wrapped around his body. He was obviously suffering from exposure and a serious wound to one foot. A blood-soaked bandage poked through a hole in one of his boots.

Duncan realised at once that he had done a dreadful thing. He may have thought he was in the presence of the Bodach, but he had been the cause of this poor creature losing his horse many miles from any civilised place.

'What're ye called?'

'Ewan Carr.' He spat the name out defiantly.

Duncan recognised him now: this was the impudent fellow who had challenged him at the waterfall.

'You're the student of Forbes, aye? Where is he?'

'How do you know about him?'

'We'll come to that later.' Duncan took a good look at him. Carr would not survive long if he didn't get to shelter. 'Help me find my pony, and then come with me. I'll make sure you're fed and warm.'

'I shall do no such thing. I must return to Blair Atholl and see the Duke.'

Duncan laughed. 'Wi' no horse, and a gunshot wound to the foot? Aye, right.'

Carr's haughty expression crumbled. He gave a sigh. 'Do what you must do. I'm too tired and cold to care.'

They examined the horse. It had expired at last and lay silent. As Duncan helped the injured man walk the two hundred yards back to the shelter, a single thought plagued him. It had troubled his conscience more than once over the last few days but now it grew to push all other concerns aside.

What has become of Professor Forbes?

* * *

By the time Duncan returned at last to the shelter with Floraidh and Ewan Carr, darkness had claimed the landscape and only the faintest glimmer of natural light showed against the snow. He made his way back by instinct more than anything else, following the burn uphill and keeping the north wind on his right cheek. Floraidh plodded at half her usual pace. She hung her head low and strained under the weight of Carr, who slumped against her neck, flitting in and out of consciousness.

Albert emerged from the gloom; a sodden shape, coat flapping in the wind, limping perhaps from damp feet or a blister. When he saw Floraidh's burden he hurried forward to help.

'Who is this? *Mein Gott!* Is he ill?'

'Exposure, sir, and a gunshot wound. He'll nae last long without fire and food.'

Duncan hoped his tone conveyed sufficient reproval. He had grown to respect the Prince, but nothing would change his opinion about what had happened at the Falls of Tarf. The Duke's order to open fire at a retreating man had been as inexplicable as it was unforgivable—and Albert had done nothing to challenge the order, which his Jaeger had gleefully carried out. In Duncan's opinion the token punishment of sending Isaac away from the hunt did not fit the crime.

Now the Prince had the goodness to look ashamed. 'Perhaps God has put this man into our care so that we may do some good. Have we any fuel?'

'Maybe if we break up Floraidh's wicker panniers.'

They hurried back to the shelter. Duncan's father sat calmly behind the shelter of the wall, rifle held loosely in one hand, the other resting on a whisky flask as he scanned the darkness for signs of movement. Smoke streamed from his pipe. Only a slight trembling of his shoulders betrayed the fact that he was just as cold and miserable as the rest of them. He looked up and grunted when he saw the others arrive.

'Well done, lad—you found her…' Then he noticed the unconscious man atop the pony, and his fingers curled around the barrel of his gun. 'Who's that?'

'Ewan Carr.' He swallowed, but his throat was dry. 'I … I shot his horse.'

McAdie stared at him as though he had sprouted a pair of antlers. 'Why d'ye do that? Dinnae tell me you were feart? A forester needs a clear head, not one stuffed full o' tales and nonsense.'

'But father—'

'Wheesht! I've had enough. You'll listen to what I have to say for once! You are a wilful, selfish boy. If you hadnae brought these strangers into the estate we would have brought the hart to bay long ago.'

'Be silent, both of you!' Albert barked. 'While you argue this man may be dying. Give him some whisky and get a fire going.'

Together they lifted the man down and lay him on the driest patch of ground in the lee of the wall. Carr blinked and shook his head before lapsing back to unconsciousness. His face was so pale that for a moment Duncan feared he had already succumbed.

While Albert wrapped the invalid in dry blankets, Duncan busied himself with Floraidh's panniers, emptying their bundled contents onto the ground before detaching the wicker baskets and smashing them up as best he could. An axe would do the job better—the willow stalks were very tough—but within a minute or two he had a stack of relatively dry wood, protected by oil from the waterproof package wrappings (the driest of which Duncan put to use as kindling).

A charge of black powder and a rifle cap ignited a hearty blaze. All crowded around the heat, all the more mindful of the cold and dark outside the shelter. McAdie upended the whisky flask into Carr's mouth and the young man spluttered, coughed, then thrashed about on the ground, awake again in an instant.

'Gad! What the devil—?'

Awareness of his situation must have returned, for Carr lay still within seconds, breathing shallowly, watching his captors with a gaze that flitted nervously from face to face.

'Be silent,' Albert commanded in a tone that would permit no disagreement.

Carr tried to rise. 'But I must find the Duke!'

Albert laid a hand on his shoulder, gently holding him down. 'Lie still! Be thankful you are still alive.' He sat back and stroked his beard, watching the young man, then smiled. 'You have led us on quite a chase, you and your companion. You ruined my hunt back at the ford, and again last night when you frightened the hart away from Glen Geusachan, but for all that I find that I like you now that I have finally seen you man to man.'

Carr merely looked bewildered at this royal condescension. Did he even realise the full effects of his actions, Duncan wondered? Did this young fool from Edinburgh know how much depended on the outcome of this hunt?

'I may have lost my hart,' Albert continued, 'but perhaps if we survive the night we will look back on these events with pride when we are old. It has been—I know not the English word—quite *ein Abenteuer*.'

'Adventure?' McAdie suggested.

'*Ja, genau.*'

Duncan hadn't thought about it in that way. "Adventure" was a concept he was aware of only in an abstract sense. It was an indulgence of the rich. The lives of the elite were devoid of physical danger, and so they felt the baffling need to reintroduce it in a controlled fashion: to hunt game for pleasure, to climb mountains for no reason, to explore the barren and distant places of the world. No ordinary man would do these things without good reason. Life was filled with quite enough hardship without wanting to create more.

He glanced at his father, whose brows were knitted together in a deep frown. He rolled his eyes at Duncan and tutted: a private look that said "Ha!—The strange ways of the nobles." Duncan smiled back, but suddenly felt very sad. This shared moment, this connection with his father, made him tremble. He looked away to hide the tears he feared he would shed if his father said a word to him now.

For years he had resented the old man, yet now he saw a trace of the father he had loved and admired as a child.

Is leaving home always this hard?

Ewan Carr seemed to be recovering. He sat up, supported himself on his elbows, and looked at Prince Albert with a grave expression. Duncan had not exchanged more than a few words with this youth, but he had seen enough to guess at his character: flighty, dramatic, prone to bursts of energy and snap decisions. This was not one of those moments. He had the look of a man who had seen the error of his ways.

'I'm obliged to you all. I've been a fool, I see that now.'

Albert brushed the words away with a wave of his hand. 'Duncan tells me you had a companion, a man of science who is making a survey of these hills. Where is he?'

Carr gestured into the darkness. 'Somewhere up there. He was quite happy when I left him.'

'Alone?'

'Alone, yes—but don't worry, Forbes is the toughest man I have ever known. He has spent months camping on glaciers in harsher weather than this.'

McAdie, who had been content to watch and listen silently, butted into the conversation with a laugh. 'Not up here, laddie. These hills make corpses o' the best of us.'

'I assure you, Forbes is quite safe.'

Duncan shook his head. This was all wrong. Carr conjured an image of an indefatigable Professor who could withstand any hardship. The reality was that his failing body could no longer keep up with the demands of his spirit.

The time had come to act.

He stood up and faced the gale. Icy pellets battered against his face, and he turned to shield his eyes from the storm. Duncan knew that if he didn't do this, nobody else would.

'Forbes willnae last the night. I'm going to find him.'

Startled faces looked up, illuminated by the feeble light of their fire. His father was the first to speak. The look in his eyes was one of fear for the safety of his only son.

'Ye'll do nothing o' the sort. Have ye lost your senses?'

'Nothing you say will dissuade me, father. I have to do this.'

McAdie shook his head and muttered something inaudible. He struggled to his feet, haggard and weary at last.

'I'm coming wi'ye, then.'

There was a fierce devotion in McAdie's scowl. His father may not be the sort of man who could easily put words to his feelings, but Duncan was beginning to understand that his actions conveyed those feelings just as powerfully, even if Duncan was usually too blind and self-centred to see it.

The mountains are the best teachers—so his father had once said.

Together they struck out into the storm.

* * *

Forbes drifted in and out of consciousness.

The mountain roared and thundered all around him. In his lucid moments, flashes of panic cut through the mist that bound his faculties and dulled his senses. *I cannot simply lie here; I must get up and move about! This is how men die of exposure!* ... Then the mist would blow in once again and he would float off into his dreams.

He was in the Alps.

A chamois stood on a rock by the side of the waterfall, head cocked to one side, staring at him with an inquisitive look. After a moment the creature tensed and jumped, landing with perfect poise on a ledge of rock the width of a man's arm. Its badger-striped face turned upwards, scanning the route to the top of the cliff, and in a series of calculated bounds it climbed a hundred feet of near-vertical rock. Stones tumbled from the ledges, some splashing into the pool by the side of the fall, others plummeting hundreds of feet to the glacier below.

Auguste Balmat, his guide, grinned and pointed to the notch in the skyline where the chamois had disappeared. The sun had been up no longer than an hour but already its blaze was fierce and Forbes felt the back of his neck starting to burn.

'That is our route, Monsieur.'

'Up there?'

A heartbeat—the whisper of wind through the grass at Montanvert—and Forbes found himself at the summit, looking down on the glacier below. Balmat pointed with his alpenstock at the peaks lining the horizon on all sides, most of them unclimbed, many without names, all terrible to the human eye: a fantastic carnival of jagged shapes, clothed in the eternal ice that Forbes had travelled so far to study.

A world of adventure waited for those with the courage to explore it.

A lucid thought interrupted his dreaming mind: *This is not at all how it was. I recall that day was cloudy.*

The sun beat down on their backs and Forbes took out his sketchbook to record the scene, making an imprint of the structures and patterns he could not have observed when on the glacier's surface. The rippled pattern of dirt bands on the ice had been observed before but never explained.

Colour and noise confused the scene, and all of a sudden he was deep in a crevasse, being lowered in jerks and stops by a different guide, years earlier. Water droplets pattered on his cap and glistened like jewels in a shaft of sunlight. Deeper—darker. A match flared. The withered skull of a man long dead, a man from another century, looked back at him. A fragment of wood from De Saussure's ladder in his pocket.

The words from letters he had written to Agassiz flashed through his mind as it made connections, burned through old memories, seeking some resolution.

You have stolen my research and profited from it. I demand you publish a retraction instantaneously.

If you do not cease your attempts then I shall endeavour to destroy you utterly in the professional sense; I have no scruples & will stop at NOTHING to correct the wrong you have done to me.

There can be no peace between us. My name is tarnished forever.

Then came the terrible night when he had come close to killing himself.

He sat quite still at his desk for two hours, churning over the conflict with Agassiz in his mind, watching the stub of a candle burn down and spill wax on his books. *I showed so much promise as a youth, but now my reputation is but a memory and Agassiz enjoys the recognition I alone merit. All has come to nothing after all.* The room where he spent so much of his life was a cold and cheerless place: a shrine to science, devoid of any decoration or human touch. He sometimes wondered if Alicia thought his soul was just as barren.

Years of illness and absence from his beloved mountains had reduced some aspect of his spirit until his brain felt like a computing machine, an engine operated by a tin man.

The knife pressed into the soft part of his thumb, drawing forth a line of blood, but cut no deeper than that.

Alicia, the next day: 'What has become of you, James? What has become of the poet I fell in love with, the man who wandered the Scottish hills and sang lullabies as the sun set over Loch Lomond? Now you labour in your study for twenty hours a day and barely speak to me when you return. You've grown cold.'

He had no answer for her. Life was very brief; he had grown up in the company of tragedy, and an impatient rhythm had beat in his breast ever since his young mind had turned to science, rebelled against the legal career chosen for him by his father. *I must become all I am capable of being, and as quickly as possible, because I will die soon.* Somehow the years had warped his zeal for life into something more proud and jealous: a desperate thirst for achievement and self-elevation, but he had lost perspective along the way. Somehow he had become so wrapped up in his obsessive battle with Agassiz that he had lost sight of what truly mattered.

What did he seek?

Agassiz was defeated—he had fled to America, unable to withstand the retaliation of his rival—and yet Forbes continued to fight, to strive to be the first and the best, to be the dominant name in his field. He worked and wore himself out, ruined his health; and for what? Was this what he had really wanted when he took his first steps into the world of science as a wide-eyed youth, reverent and humble before the glories of Nature?

Ewan Carr: 'Your career was made long ago. You just don't appreciate what you have.'

The gearbox of his mind had processed its data and come to a terrible conclusion. Self-awareness flooded in, illuminating the sins of hypocrisy and pride that had driven his actions for so many years.

'What am I doing here?' he said aloud, and opened his eyes.

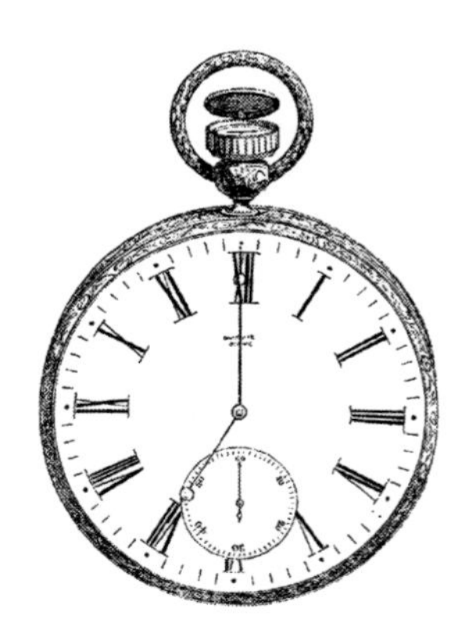

CHAPTER VII
ESCAPE

DUNCAN CROUCHED NEXT TO the low stone wall that partially shielded the sprawled form of Professor Forbes from the wind. His father stood behind him with the candle lamp. The flame leapt with every gust, making Duncan's shadow dance a crazy jig against the blur of incoming snowflakes.

'Is he alive?'

The Professor's eyes were open. He stared into the darkness, perhaps by now looking at the vistas of another world. Duncan knelt by his side and laid a hand on his shoulder, disturbing the layer of snow that had built up there—and yet some warmth remained.

'Forbes?'

McAdie took a step forward and crouched next to him. Duncan couldn't see his father's face, but he allowed himself to imagine that the old man looked on the scene with compassion instead of his usual scowl.

'Maybe it's too late, son.'

'Do you no see? It's my fault this has happened. I shouldnae have left him at the Falls of Tarf.'

'You did your duty. Your loyalty is to the Duke, to the estate, not to him.'

'But I broke my word!'

His father said nothing to that.

Duncan felt movement under his hand. Forbes murmured something and rolled over, dislodging the snow which had built up on his jacket; then he began to shiver violently and curled up into a tight ball, wrapping his arms around his head.

'He's alive! Quick, father, help me get him up!'

McAdie put the lantern down and took hold of the Professor's boots while Duncan grabbed him by the shoulders. Forbes was surprisingly light, but his restless movements made him an awkward package to carry.

They had gone perhaps fifty yards when he suddenly convulsed and let out a shout. The lantern dropped and smashed on a rock, extinguishing their sole light source. Duncan shivered while his father swore in the darkness. He felt terribly cold and worn out, and although his fear of the Bodach had been vanquished he could not shake a sense of apprehension.

Then Forbes spoke: 'What am I doing here?'

Both men who carried him stopped in surprise.

'Are ye awake?' McAdie demanded. 'Can ye walk, or are we to continue hauling you through the dark until we fall to our deaths who knows where?'

Duncan could feel the convulsions now shuddering through the Professor's body. God only knew how cold the poor man must be.

'I think I can stand.'

They lowered him to the ground, Duncan rather more gently than his father. Forbes sat for a moment, motionless, before standing and looking at his rescuers with eyes that glinted in the meagre light available.

'Is that you, Duncan?'

He sounded frail, vulnerable. Duncan took a moment to analyse his feelings, and realised the overwhelming emotion he felt at this exact moment was one of gratitude that he had been given the chance to do the right thing after all.

'Aye, it's me.'

'I'm most … most dreadfully cold. Catch me if I fall again, will you?' His voice faltered and he stumbled, reaching out to grab Duncan's arm. 'Something has happened to me. I'll be all right in a bit. Only catch me if I fall…'

Duncan and his father steadied him between them, taking an arm apiece and moving downhill one steady step at a time. Duncan's eyes had begun to adapt to the darkness. He could make out nothing but indistinct shapes close to, and the greater expanse of sky, an infinitesimally lighter shade of grey than the mountain; but his other senses attempted to compensate, and with every breath he detected the faint but unmistakable aroma of the camp fire they were trying to find. Sounds, too, supplied a wealth of information. The burn roared to their right, swollen by rain and melting snow. Wind whistled through a gap in the cliffs a thousand feet above.

'Left … straight on there … right a bit, laddie.' His father's instructions were confident as he guided them away from hazards and downhill towards safety.

Soon a spark flickered in the distance—at first so faint it might easily be a trick of the eyes, but within minutes Duncan could tell that it was the campfire where Prince Albert and Ewan Carr were sheltering from the weather.

* * *

While the others tried to sleep, Duncan kept watch.

He rested his hand against the hammer of his rifle and gazed out into the mist, paler now that the longest hours of the night had passed. He prodded the remains of the fire with the toe of his boot but it had long since burned down, leaving a mess of black sludge and unburned sticks.

The air smelled of autumn: damp moss, peat, the musty scent of rotting heather stalks. He could feel the imminent change of season with some sense he possessed more subtle than sight or smell, an impulse not unlike the forces that draw the stags down from the mountains to bellow and fight each other in the morning mist. *As the landscape breathes out at the end of its short summer, so the little lives it nurtures are compelled to dance to its ancient rhythm. So it has always been.*

Duncan understood why his father felt such a spiritual connection to this land. When one is a part of it—truly a part of it—every running stag, every burn in spate, every ripple of wind in the grass creates an echo in the spirit of the man. Some chose to call it God. Duncan's father did not call it anything at all, and yet he felt it powerfully and relied on this connection, this kinship, to guide his footsteps every day of his life.

On a morning like this, when Duncan was thankful simply to be alive, he began to believe he could feel it too. For a long time he had resisted this immersion in the landscape, fearing he would become his father and make the same mistakes, miss the same opportunities. Not until today did he wonder if perhaps it was worth it after all.

The snow melted as daybreak approached. Clumps of it dropped from the heather, pattering on the ground to compose an eerie dawn chorus. Patches of darker ground burst through the coating of white on the crown of the mountain. By the time the first watery light of dawn glinted from beneath the cloud in the east, only the very top of the cliffs still held any new snow; the swiftly rising temperatures had destroyed the rest.

At last, a sense of peace returned to the mountain. The wind had exhausted itself, the snows were melting, and the old silence returned to the hidden bowl of An Garbh-choire.

Albert was the first to wake. He stirred beneath his blanket, then an arm appeared, fumbling blindly for his rifle. Only when he had a firm grasp on the barrel did he look out from under the cover and cast a wary glance around the campsite.

'Good morning, sir,' Duncan ventured.

Albert seemed not to hear him. He sniffed the air, pulled on his boots, and stood up.

'The weather is clear! We must leave at once. Victoria will never forgive me if we delay for another moment.'

His cry roused the others. Duncan's father stifled a yawn, no doubt intending to convey the impression that he had not slept at all. He sniffed the air, glanced around the interior of the corrie, and shook the droplets from his jacket. Forbes and Carr, buried under a bundle of blankets next to what remained of the fire, stirred but did not get up. Duncan had watched them carefully through the night and was glad both had finally managed to get some rest.

Albert crouched beside them and looked up at Duncan. 'How are they?'

'They slept like bairns. I widnae worry about them, sir.'

Carr was the first to rise. He crawled out from under the blanket and sat up on a rock, picking at the dressing on his foot. Duncan could not claim an intimate acquaintance, but he had marked him as a high spirited, fast burning sort of fellow. This morning he was unusually silent.

'Don't pick at the bandage,' Albert commanded. 'I did not put myself to such trouble last night—while, need I add, you were fighting for your life—only for you to discard it now.'

Carr turned his head slowly, as if he heard Albert through a great depth of water.

'It hurts.'

Duncan's father, who had remained characteristically silent, interrupted the conversation. He pushed past Duncan and took Albert to one side, conferring with him in anxious tones.

Just then Duncan realised what his father had smelled: the faint whiff of infection.

Carr did not resist as McAdie peeled back the bandage and inspected the injury. The bullet had struck the day before yesterday, and all attempts at treatment since had been hurried and undertaken in trying conditions: heat, damp, miasma, then finally drenching rain and cold. Few battlefields were as harsh to a wounded man as the Cairngorms. It would take a superhuman to ward off infection under such circumstances.

McAdie drew back with a sharp intake of breath. 'Ach! He'll nae last the day.'

'That is not an acceptable answer,' Albert said. 'I do not intend the outcome of this expedition to be any worse than we can help. This man is in my care and I will not lose him.'

'But his wound's gone bad! I've seen it more than once. We'll nae find a doctor in time.'

'What is the shortest route to civilisation?'

McAdie paused before replying. 'Why should we help him? Tell me that, sir, an' I'll do whatever ye ask o' me.'

'Because we are human beings, and I am not like your master; that much is clear.' Albert's expression conveyed a warning that McAdie was treading on dangerous ground. 'Now tell me what is the best route to a doctor!'

McAdie grunted. 'South.'

Albert nodded. 'Thank you. Now, Duncan, get the Professor up and see how he is, then pack our things.'

Duncan reached down and shook Forbes gently. The Professor lay curled up in a ball beneath the blankets, arms wrapped protectively around his head. A few wispy strands of hair stirred in the breeze. He looked very frail this morning.

'Sir? It's a braw morning. Time to break our fast.'

Forbes opened his eyes and looked up at Duncan. That expression! Duncan saw a vast depth of sorrow in those eyes: a lifetime of fears and regrets, compounded by the weight of some awful realisation. The ineffable spark that had first drawn Duncan to him, that hint of greatness, had gone. The wistful poet's glance, the shrewd and calculating intelligence of the master scientist, the determination to overcome his own physical deficiencies: these qualities had all disappeared.

'Duncan...' he said in a weak voice. 'God bless you, my boy. I knew you had an honest soul.'

'Can ye forgive me, sir? I shouldnae have left ye at the Tarf water.'

'There is nothing to forgive. You were there when it mattered, unlike my absent student.' His expression darkened. 'Carr abandoned me, would you believe it? In his condition! In such weather!'

'Aye, I ken. He's here.'

'Here? By God, I will have it out with him.'

The Professor struggled to his feet, but the effort momentarily overcame his faculties and he slumped against Duncan in a swoon. Duncan knew little of medical matters but he recognised serious illness when he saw it.

'We must get ye both to a doctor, sir. You're nae well.'

'I am dying, you fool,' Forbes said through gritted teeth. 'This expedition was to be my last great moment as a field geologist.'

'But why put yourself through all this, if you're dying?'

'It is precisely because I have not long to live that I must do it. I'm alive yet, by God, and while I still breathe I shall not submit.' He looked at Duncan calmly. 'I don't fear death, my boy. I fear not having lived to my full potential.'

And there, in a few words, Duncan saw the Professor's true nature shine through once again. Duncan understood nothing of science or geology, but he recognised the light when he saw it.

He asked himself if he still believed in the Bodach. It was not an easy question to answer, but of one thing he was absolutely certain: ever since he had stood up to his fear and gone out there into the snow and the storm, these mountains no longer filled him with superstitious terror. He had Forbes to thank for opening his eyes.

* * *

Victoria scanned the hillside for any sign of her husband. She had spent a miserable night in the shelter of a ruined croft, and had quite unfairly abused Thomas over the weather and the wickedness of her absent husband. Now she had but one desire: to find Albert and bring him home.

Fortunately the weather had brightened with every league they had ridden north. Now the sun was burning off last night's peppering of snow, although she observed that some hollows, high on the hill and concealed from the sun's rays, remained frozen.

To think that poor Albert was forced to spend the night out here in the wild, away from the consolation of his family, or even a roof over his head!

Her feelings oscillated between concern and indignant fury. Their marriage was based on mutually negotiated rules—an informal contract that existed for the benefit and happiness of them both. Albert knew better than to try to impose his will on her; on her part, Victoria understood that her husband had to feel important and useful in order to be happy. She had given him power and responsibilities, projects to manage, the opportunity to roam and hunt in the wild. In return he did not try to control her or go against her will. It had taken years to get right, but this arrangement had built a marriage of firm foundations.

Now Albert had broken one of those rules. In her moments of fury, she imagined scolding him in front of his foresters before storming off alone; and yet five minutes later she would be consumed with worry for his safety, thinking the best of him—that perhaps he was not hunting Professor Forbes after all and that it had all been some monstrous mistake.

The only thing she knew for certain was that she could not imagine another day without him.

She heard a shout from Thomas, and looked up to see Isaac running through the heather towards them, hunched over in imitation of the stooped run of the foresters. He carried his telescope in his right hand and his gun slung across his back. As he halted before Victoria's pony she observed that his face was slick with sweat and he was breathing heavily from the exertion.

'*Meine Königen,* Albert is less than a mile away on the other side of that ridge.'

'Have you seen him?' she demanded. 'Is he well?'

'I have seen him only at a distance. He is well enough to walk.'

'Take me to him directly.'

Isaac bowed and led the way. Victoria felt like spurring her pony on and galloping to meet her husband—to scold him or embrace him, she didn't quite know which just yet—but she resisted the temptation. *I shall ride this last mile calmly and with dignity,* she thought, *and deny him the satisfaction of seeing his poor wife in hysterics.*

Nevertheless, she found herself pressing her heels into the flanks of her pony and wishing the last mile could be reduced to a few yards.

* * *

The mountain is letting us go, Duncan thought as they left the bowl of An Garbh-choire and found themselves once again in the deep trench of Glen Dee. The river carried its load of meltwater south. Its ceaseless roar was the only sound the ear could detect in that otherwise silent place. As they paused for a rest beneath a cataract that flowed down gigantic slabs from the mountain above, Duncan was seized by a powerful emotion that gripped his soul for a moment before departing once again. Was it relief that they had survived until now, an echo of lingering fear, or worry about the journey ahead? Was it an instinctive expression of awe at the vast scale of the landscape through which they voyaged? Duncan didn't know, but he clung to the emotion in much the same way that a benighted shepherd is drawn to the lights of a friendly shieling.

I am human, puny within the vast splendour of Nature. That is all there is.

All his life he had probed the boundaries of his world, searched for an escape, dreamed of a life beyond. His father was troubled by none of these fantasies. Frustrated ambition may have tainted his happiness, but when on the hill he let all of that go and found contentment in his relationship with the landscape that both nurtured him and regularly threatened his life.

But I am young and impatient … I could never live in such a way, not until I am old.

So Duncan thought, and yet when he looked up at the cataract, which had flowed down those slabs and crashed into the boulders at the bottom without pause for aeons, he felt drawn back into this timeless world by a force more inexorable than anything which pushed him away.

He looked south, down the long miles of Glen Dee, and saw a gigantic hart standing atop one of the knolls by the river. Damh-mor seemed to be waiting for them, or perhaps leading them away from An Garbh-choire. Duncan wondered who was truly the hunter in this expedition, and who was playing with whom.

Instantly he dropped to the ground, and his father, noticing the movement, did likewise.

'What d'ye see, laddie?' his father whispered.

'It's the beastie, up ahead! A hundred paces, maybe more.'

A look of excitement crossed Albert's face for a moment before being replaced by a more subdued expression. He glanced at the invalids. 'Surely we cannot spare the time. Every moment is precious if we are to save them.'

'It willnae take long,' McAdie pressed. 'Sir, this is our last chance.'

Professor Forbes, who had sat down on the nearest rock to rest while they discussed the matter, shrugged his shoulders. He still looked old and tired but had regained a small measure of vitality, enough at least to limp alongside the pony.

'Do what you will; this is not our expedition. All I ask is that you don't forget us.'

Albert nodded his thanks. McAdie ordered Forbes to stay well back with Carr and the pony, then crawled forward to join the others in the heather. Now that his conscience was appeased, Albert clutched his rifle and had a look of wild enthusiasm about him. Duncan could not shake a sense that the hart was toying with them, leading them on a chase for the fun of it; but he had no doubt that Albert would do his best.

'Tell me what to do, McAdie.'

'Follow me, be silent, and make your shot count this time.'

They crawled forward, staying below the level of the heather but occasionally pausing to get a better view of their quarry. Damh-mor stood guard on the top of his mound, munching a heather shoot. Duncan noticed that the beast held one leg aloft, and when he took a few steps to one side he moved with a limp.

'He's lame, father.'

'Aye, I ken. Albert will have an easy shot this time.'

McAdie looked triumphant. A forester takes great pride in his work, and none more than Alec McAdie. If he could make a success of this hunt after everything that had gone wrong, perhaps the Duke would look favourably on him after all. It could all be turned around. He would be head keeper after all these years.

However, Albert looked troubled.

'The beast is lame? How?'

McAdie shrugged. 'The corries are dangerous places for a hart.'

Over the next ten minutes they continued to manoeuvre, bringing themselves around so that they were downwind of the target, negotiating their position, selecting a ridge of high ground amongst the hummocks and knolls of heathery rubble beside the River Dee. Damh-mor's hillock lay less than forty yards away, and the stag cut a sharp silhouette against the sky. McAdie had lined up a perfect shot for Prince Albert. This time he could not possibly miss.

Now that they had moved closer, Duncan could clearly see that Damh-mor was in a sorry condition. His coat had looked bedraggled when they had spied him before, but now it was positively matted with peat and mire—a black and crusty mess, streaked with blood from his wound. Had he fallen into a bog and struggled to get out again, injuring his leg in the process? Even from this distance it was obvious that his left foreleg was maimed by an open gash. The beast stood in a hunched posture, legs shaking, hardly able to keep his head upright under the massive weight of his antlers.

Duncan realised at once that the hart was not in control at all. He was an animal of flesh and bone, not a supernatural being who could influence the fate of men. The monarch of these hills had been reduced to a pitiful condition by the humans who had hunted him for many miles, chased him out of his usual territory and into the ice corries where many pitfalls awaited even the most sure-footed hart.

Duncan noticed riders approaching along the riverbank from the south. The rider in front wore a brown travelling dress and rode on a side saddle: a lady, then!

He pointed. McAdie twitched his telescope in the direction of the travellers and uttered a curse in Gaelic.

'Strangers! Ach, damn them—they'll ruin everything. Sir, we must take our shot now.'

Albert hesitated. He ran a hand down the stock of his rifle, brushing past the lock as if exploring the idea of pulling it back and making it ready for a shot; but he left it where it was, and didn't raise the piece to his shoulder.

'They'll be here in moments, sir!' McAdie urged. His face was steadily turning red with frustration and anger. 'In the name o' Christ … damn ye, will ye nae take the shot? We've come all this way, and it's as easy as shooting a scarecrow at this range! The beast couldnae run if he wanted to.'

'That is precisely the problem. Now that it comes to it—well, look at him. Look at what we have done to him.'

'If we'd have shot him yesterday he'd be dead and gralloched and packed on Floraidh's back by now, on the way to the master's kitchens.'

'There is a great difference between shooting an animal in a sporting manner—a battle between equals, as it were—and a base slaughter. In my country sometimes it is seen to be more honourable not to pull the trigger.'

Such was McAdie's apoplexy that he merely opened his mouth, unable to voice a coherent reply.

'The riders are nearly here,' Duncan warned. He had been keeping an eye on the strangers while his father argued his point with the Prince, and now that they were almost upon them a suspicion began to grow in his mind. Who could this lady be, and why did she ride with such haste towards them?

A cry echoed through the valley: 'Albert! Albert, it's me!'

Damh-mor tensed, sniffed the air, but did not run. In the space of a moment Albert's expression changed from indecision to horror. A gentleman will sometimes go hunting when his wife is a member of the party, perhaps riding a little way behind, but his behaviour will not be the same. He will moderate his language, be more courteous in his discourse with the servants, and perhaps display a little less savagery in his pursuit of the hart. Albert already knew he was in trouble with his wife, both for missing his birthday celebrations and for staying out on the hill far longer than originally agreed.

'By all that is holy, Victoria is here!'

By this point McAdie could barely contain his anger. 'Get rid of her, sir. At once.'

Albert's eyes flashed in response. 'Be careful how you speak, McAdie. That is my wife you refer to—and your sovereign.'

'By God, sir, at this moment she is a hindrance to my stalk, and I willnae have it, d'ye hear me?' He shot a vicious look at Duncan. 'Go and explain the situation to the Queen, laddie.'

Duncan opened his mouth to refuse the order, but at that moment he feared his father more than the Queen. Taking care to move quickly and quietly, he slithered away to try and persuade the Queen to be quiet and turn around.

* * *

Duncan had spent enough time in the company of Prince Albert for his initial sense of awe to have faded. He found himself able to talk to Albert, if not as an equal then as master and servant.

However, he felt nothing but dread at the prospect of addressing the Queen.

What shall I say? How shall I introduce myself?

She rode on a Highland pony not unlike Floraidh, but a stallion—*aigeach*—instead of a mare. The Queen must have spent the night in the wild, but nevertheless she radiated an indefinable aura of elegance and privilege. A veiled hat perched on her head, and her slightly plump cheeks were rosy from the breeze. She gripped the reins with gloved hands. Long tartan skirts, streaked with mud, protected her legs from the wind and rain.

A look of determination burned in those eyes. She must have caught sight of Duncan, for she turned her pony and spurred him to a canter.

'You, there! Boy!'

He stood and waited for her to draw near. He could not help trembling a little. Isaac and Thomas, he noticed, trailed some distance behind.

He took off his cap and bowed as she drew to a halt a few yards away.

'Your Majesty—' he began.

'Where is Prince Albert?'

He found himself unable to meet her gaze for fear of melting into a puddle on the ground. He wished she would dismount so they could at least speak at the same level, but she remained in her saddle, looking down her nose at him.

He cleared his throat. *This is it; I'll be lucky if she doesn't order me shot where I stand. Isaac would take pleasure in it.*

'I must respectfully ask ye to proceed no further, Ma'am. Albert is lining up his shot the now, an' it widnae do for him to be disturbed.'

For a moment he thought the Queen would explode with anger and ride him down, but the moment passed and the rage faded in her eyes, to be replaced by a calmer appraisal of the facts.

'He has had his sport. I am tired of waiting for him to return to the castle, and if he cannot spare a few moments to speak to his poor wife after the trying journey I have had, then—well!'

Duncan despaired of being able to persuade her. 'Will ye no consider, Ma'am—?'

'I have considered! Are you married?'

He shook his head.

'No? Well, you shall be one day, and then perhaps you will understand.'

With that she took the reins into her hands and rode past him, aiming for the low rise where Albert and McAdie were hidden amongst the heather. Isaac thundered past on his horse moments later.

* * *

Forbes glanced at his pocket watch—which was, against all odds, still ticking—and calculated that almost half an hour had passed since he, Carr, and the pony had been ordered to lie down on the ground and "Haud yer wheesht!" until somebody should come back and retrieve them. The pony seemed quite content to lie on her belly, nibble stalks of heather, and breathe heavily down the back of his neck. He had attempted to move, but the ground was rocky here and nowhere else was comfortable.

Of course, he had given Albert permission to proceed with the hunt and damn the consequences. What else could he do? Perhaps a week ago he could have mustered the courage to say no, to thwart the will of the Prince, but much had happened since then. He was too tired and cold, too beaten down by everything that had happened to do anything else.

Nevertheless, some tiny pocket of resistance stood firm and objected to how they were being treated.

'I have had enough of this,' he muttered, then turned to see how his student was faring.

Carr slumped against one of the makeshift provision sacks tied to the pony's flank. He had regained some semblance of consciousness, intermittently at least, but his condition remained very bad. The poor boy's face was shockingly pale, his lips thin and drawn back, eyes dry and staring. He frequently groped for the nearest flask and gulped down mouthfuls of whisky. Now that he had lost his boot with the bullet hole in it, Forbes could not help but stare at the clumsy ball of makeshift bandage wrapped around his injured foot, stained brown with blood. It had proven quite impossible to change bandages as frequently as they ought to, for they had run out of clean clothes to cut into rags.

On several occasions, Carr had grinned stoically and tried to muster a joke—something in the order of "Beats the monotony of town!" or "Something for a lecture at the Royal Society, eh?" The gloom and despair of last night had disappeared with the dawn, but Forbes recognised the crumbling defences of a beaten man.

Despite his anger with the boy for abandoning him, an overpowering weight of guilt had settled on his shoulders. When combined with his new awareness of how he had abused his life and his gifts, the cocktail of despair was a potent brew and it made him want to curl up under a rock and never emerge.

The minutes passed in an agony of self-recrimination. He hardly dared look at his poor student. Every moment spent grovelling amongst the heather and the rocks was a moment in which Carr's strength faded a little more, and a happy outcome became a little less likely. Prince Albert and the foresters had promised to return, but now that they were away stalking their prize they had probably forgotten all about the invalids. Besides, when the dead stag was placed on the pony's back, where would Carr ride? Would he be forced to walk the long miles in his deteriorating condition?

'I have had enough,' he said again, louder this time.

He made up his mind. If the others placed greater importance on a stag than on the lives of their fellow men, then it was time to leave them behind and try to find help alone.

I want to be back at Eastertyre with my wife and daughters. The emotion flitted unbidden across his mind, but it was a powerful feeling and for a moment he thought it would overwhelm him.

No more distractions. Forbes would take his student to a doctor and then take the shortest road home to his family. His little adventure was at an end; it was time to wake up to the reality of his responsibilities. He could not rely on Prince Albert or the foresters to take them to safety.

'We're leaving. Get back on the pony, and be quiet about it. I don't know how long the others will be.'

He helped Carr up onto the pony's back, taking care not to damage the precious supplies of food that remained. Forbes stood up slowly and scanned the horizon, looking for any signs of the others. All was quiet save the roar of the river.

He felt so dreadfully, horribly tired. Could he walk the distance? He had to try.

'Isn't this theft?' Carr asked as the pony started to pick her way between the rocks.

'At this point, my boy, I don't care.'

Carr attempted a laugh, but it came out more like a splutter. 'Is it not your usual habit to attempt to drum moral values into my head? How very unlike you.'

'This is more serious than right or wrong. Our lives are at risk.'

'I know.' Carr's tone was serious again. 'For God's sake, I'm trying to stay cheerful. Heaven knows I have little enough to look forward to if … if I live through this.'

Forbes thought of all the advice he could give the boy, about perseverance, realistic expectations, the value of hard work and honesty, but now was not the time.

He led the pony by the reins over the brow of a small rise, and to his shock was almost run down by three riders. The first was a lady in fine clothes, riding a shaggy Highland pony; the other two were men, one young and one old, both carrying rifles. He recognised the younger of the two by his German hunting hat and the sharp look in his eyes. This was the Jaeger who had attacked them at the Falls of Tarf, and now he spurred his horse in front of the lady as if to protect her, holding the reins in his left hand and brandishing his firearm in the other.

His sharp gaze was fixed on the person of Ewan Carr.

'Halt, you there! Identify yourselves!'

'Let me address them directly, Isaac,' the lady interrupted. 'I am sure there is no danger.'

'But they could be highwaymen!'

'You are too quick to identify every traveller in these hills as a poacher and a miscreant. Do stand down before another *accident* occurs.'

Isaac lowered his gun (reluctantly, Forbes thought) and steered his horse out of the way. The lady dismounted, taking care to lift her heavy skirts out of the heather. Now that she stood on the same level as Forbes, he noticed that she was not a tall lady—rather short and a little stout, if truth be told—yet she had a pleasant face and a look of shrewd intelligence about her.

It took a moment to realise that he was in the presence of Queen Victoria. He had seen pictures of her, of course, but he had simply not expected to meet her in a place like this. He had only just got used to the prospect of Prince Albert being a living human being, capable of humour and conversation; this was something else altogether.

He made a clumsy bow. 'Your Majesty, forgive me for startling you.'

She laughed, apparently delighted by the show of formality in such a wild place. 'Professor Forbes, I presume?'

'You know who I am?'

'We have been looking for you. Your wife is greatly concerned for your safety—as am I.' The Queen frowned as she looked at him more closely. 'You look unwell. And your companion! Is he injured?'

He felt another wave of trembling weakness come over him, and sat down on the nearest rock, head spinning. 'We … we are both ill, Ma'am. My student was shot and is in need of a doctor. Albert—'

Victoria's reply was instant and furious. 'Albert is responsible for this, I know he is! If only he had not believed the Duke…'

Without giving Forbes a chance to reply, she turned and mounted her pony, spurring him to a canter. The foresters followed.

'We shall return for you directly!' she called back after a moment.

'Albert saved us,' Forbes finished, too late, and shook his head in frustration.

* * *

As she climbed the final rise to the knoll where Albert was hiding amongst the heather, Victoria's mind was in turmoil. She wanted to punish him for disobeying her. She wanted to chase away his stag, embarrass him in front of the foresters, and drag him back to Blair to apologise to everyone he had inconvenienced.

Stones crunched under her boots. She crouched down low as she approached the crest of the mound.

Where is he?

Something rustled in the heather just ahead. She crawled a little further.

'Are ye nae going to announce yersel', Ma'am?'

McAdie's tone was dry, perhaps angry. She stood upright to confront the forester, expecting to find him hidden in the heather with Albert, poised to shoot the hart. An angry reaction to her presence—"you have ruined my hunt!"—would add a little spice to the row. She was looking forward to ruining his hunt; he had, after all, done his best to ruin their Scottish holiday.

To her great surprise, the two men were sitting together on a flat rock, making no attempt to conceal themselves.

McAdie looked like he always did: scruffy, bearded, face screwed up in a weathered scowl that could signify any of a hundred emotions, smoking his pipe. The only sign that he had been prone amongst the heather roots only a few minutes before was a great smear of black mud down the front of his waistcoat.

As Victoria approached, McAdie touched his cap and made his leave.

It was in Albert that Victoria noticed the greatest change. The visible strain on his countenance came as a shock to her. Stubble sprouted from his face, which was smeared with dirt and deeply lined, as if he had hardly slept for days. Both of his hands were black with mud, and his smart hunting jacket was probably too scratched, torn, and stained to be of any use after this adventure came to an end.

Yet, for all the evidence of his physical discomfort and the dangers he had endured, Albert smiled.

'Hello, *mein Lieb.*'

She flew forward and embraced him, hugging his body fiercely to her own while simultaneously striking his back with the palms of her hands, raining down blows on him.

'Oh! I could kill you, I am so angry ... but you're quite safe and well? I was so worried!'

'Victoria! Be calm, my love. I am well. Don't worry!'

She drew away for a moment, still holding him in her arms. He looked concerned and baffled at her behaviour.

'Tell me the truth. Have you come all the way out here to hunt the men who defied you at the Falls of Tarf? I have heard such things, Albert. If they are true I shall never speak to you again. I have seen Forbes and his student just now, and if you have harmed them I swear by all the power I hold—'

'Hush! Hush now; it is not true!'

'But they are in a terrible condition! I fear for their lives. You and McAdie have chased them on the advice of Murray and your bloodthirsty Jaeger, I know it. Tell me the truth, Albert.'

He shook his head, and Victoria wanted to believe him.

'We rescued them. I realised long ago they were not our enemies, although'—here he chuckled—'they have done much to obstruct my hunt. We are escorting them to safety so that doctors may tend to young Mr Carr.'

She said nothing. Looking into his eyes, she saw nothing but honesty and truth looking back at her. Perhaps it was not true after all, then … but there was still the matter of his hunt, which had taken far too long and interfered with her plans.

'Even if that is true, you have disobeyed me. You stayed out for more than a day. Think of the plans I made for your birthday celebrations, all ruined! What do you say to that? You have made me come all the way out here because the Professor's poor wife was quite mad with apprehension, and of course what could I do when I heard my husband may be acting so dishonourably? You have placed me in an awful position.'

Now at last he looked rueful. 'I am sorry. The hart ran and ran; always we thought we would catch him in another hour, or perhaps another. You should see him, Victoria! He is the most magnificent beast I have ever seen. I could not let him go, not after he had bested me.'

She felt her patience wane. At his best, Albert was the finest husband a Queen could wish for, and yet at his worst he could be just as boorish and obsessed with blood sports as any other man.

'What you mean is that you missed. You are a terrible shot, and yet you will stubbornly persist in the hope of killing some poor creature who would be better off roaming free.'

'I did not miss; at least, not the first time,' he said stiffly. 'Circumstances were against us. This was the most finely-matched contest of my sporting career.'

'Well, where is this noble stag, then? Come, show him to me.'

In truth she did not relish the prospect of being shown yet another bloody and disembowelled carcass, and yet it was expected of her to feign delight at the sight of a champion hart brought down.

'We spared him.'

That was not the answer she had expected. 'Pardon?'

'Damh-mor was half dead anyway and in a poor state. I pitied him. There would be no honour in such a slaughter, and besides, I knew you would not approve. We have had our adventure.'

It began to dawn on Victoria that her impressions of Albert's misdeeds had been all wrong.

Albert gestured towards the river. The hart was well-camouflaged, but after a moment she was able to discern the outline of a huge animal lying peacefully on a carpet of moss. His antlers were ragged and hung with tufts of grass, and mud coated his fur, but Damh-mor's eyes were open and his flank rose and fell gently with every breath.

The champion hart of Atholl was at peace and resting.

'He is beautiful,' she whispered, afraid of raising her voice in case the flighty creature ran away. 'Will he live?'

'McAdie says he may do, if he returns to his home pastures before winter.'

'I hope he does. You've done a noble thing, Albert.'

'I acted according to my conscience and my abilities. Out here where life is hard a man can do nothing more: this I have learned from my companions.'

His expression became serious, and Victoria knew that he was thinking about the lives that depended on his

"AT PEACE AND RESTING"

actions—lives he had already worked hard to save. Every dark assumption in her heart, every suspicion, had been turned around to shine a light on Albert's virtues. He was not a bloodthirsty hunter of poachers after all. His only sin was one of pride, and out of all the seven deadly sins that was the one Victoria found it the easiest to forgive.

She pulled him to his feet and kissed him, then wrinkled her nose.

'You smell.'

He laughed. 'So I am forgiven?'

'Perhaps. Come—if we are to find our way to a doctor, no hour of daylight can be spared. I shall send Isaac ahead to raise the alarm.'

She took her husband by the arm and led him back down to the path, once again calm and happy. Her thoughts turned to the pressing task of rescuing Forbes and Carr, but in her mind they were all but safe already; for once Victoria turned her will to an objective, she would accept no outcome but a good one.

I am travelling through the beautiful Highlands with Albert by my side after all. All is as it should be.

CHAPTER VIII
A NEW DAWN

THE CARAVAN OF WEARY souls reached Lochain Lodge shortly after ten o'clock that night.

Duncan had not left the Professor's side for the duration of their voyage south. It had become clear that Forbes could no longer walk safely—he was simply too exhausted, and too likely to collapse without warning—but the Queen graciously gave him the use of her own pony, Arghait Bhean. His hooves trod the long miles beside the stoic and uncomplaining Floraidh, whose resilience had impressed Duncan. He vowed to cherish that beast even more from this day on, for it was rare to find a pony who could endure so much without complaint. He patted her nose; she snorted and nuzzled against his arm.

The two invalids were conscious for more of the journey than Duncan had expected. Carr cracked jokes now and again, although in the long spells of silence Duncan saw a hopeless expression steal over the young man's face. His injured foot, wrapped up clumsily in a ball of moss in a vain attempt to fight the infection, swung uselessly at his side.

Professor Forbes often looked back over his shoulder at the receding mountains. They smiled in sunshine now, benign giants, all fearsome majesty and storm long forgotten. The Bodach was quiet once again. He had expelled the invaders and kept his secrets. Duncan wondered if Forbes felt any regret that he had been unable to answer the questions he had come here to investigate.

Victoria took the pony of Auld Thomas when it was offered, but she seemed dissatisfied with the beast. It refused to obey her instructions and often strayed from the path to nibble choice clumps of vegetation. After ten miles of irritation she declared that she would walk, and for the remainder of the voyage she strode beside her beloved Albert, often hand in hand at the rear of the column.

McAdie took the lead and stayed well in front of everybody else. Duncan wondered what thoughts might be passing through his father's mind. By any definition the hunt had been a failure, but nobody could say McAdie had not tried. He had used every skill he possessed, tried to the utmost, and yet at the end Albert had refused to take the shot.

Duncan smiled wryly. What would the Duke of Atholl say to this? Once again their future was in Prince Albert's hands.

This might be his last journey through these hills. That thought made him quiet for a long time, and as they forded the Tarf water near dusk Duncan thought he would cry. Never to see this beloved gorge again ... never again to swing on those birches! The thought could not be endured.

I will leave these hills one day, perhaps soon. But it will be at the moment of my own choosing, and I will say my goodbyes in my own way.

Victoria had lit a candle lantern as soon as the light started to fail, but the foresters knew better and they relied on their eyes alone to guide them along the road. Duncan was back on his home soil and he knew every rock, every curve of the young River Tilt, every *bealach* in the hills stark against the gloaming. The landscape narrowed, drawing in to confine them in the twisting glen many miles from Blair Atholl.

Soon Duncan's nostrils detected a faint aroma above the tang of peat and heather. He could smell the smoke of his home fire. A warm bed, a bowl of Atholl Brose, maybe a smoked trout and a bannock for supper … the promise of these things made him forget himself for a moment. His stomach emitted an audible growl and he allowed himself to feel the fatigue in his limbs—just for a moment, mind.

Looking left, he could already see his father—a faint silhouette against the bright ribbon of the river—crossing the secret ford to Glen Lochain, the wee glen where Lochain Lodge hid amongst the folds of the moors. Auld Thomas caught up with him. Duncan could hardly see him in the darkness, but knew the old man would be smiling and tireless as always.

'I wonder if we should stop the night,' Duncan thought out loud. 'Lochain Lodge is hardly fit for a Queen, though…'

'Och, she's a rare lady and nae mistake, laddie—I widnae worry too much about her. She'll weather it.'

He nodded. 'I'll tell the others.'

Duncan took hold of Floraidh's rein and whispered a command in her ear. She stopped, and Arghait Bhean stopped beside her. Carr awoke with a jolt and a cry of surprise.

Soon the royal couple caught up with them. Victoria held the lantern in her right hand while her left attempted to lift her skirts out of the mud. Albert walked with a slight limp, no doubt caused by blisters, and carried his rifle over one shoulder.

'Why have we stopped?' the Queen inquired. 'Surely every moment is of critical importance if we are to save the life of that young man.'

'Aye, Ma'am, that it is, only—'

'Well?'

'Only my house is nearby, an' my mother is a skilled healer. We could stop here the night. She could help Ewan Carr.'

'Will your mother consent to accompany us to Blair Castle? I see no reason to stop until we get there.'

That was not the answer Duncan had expected. Was she not a lady, and a royal one at that? He had expected her to be fatigued, to demand a bed for the night; in short, to create trouble for the entire party until her wishes and comforts were administered to.

'Are ye no tired, Ma'am?'

'Of course I am tired, Duncan. I expect you also are tired. My poor dear Albert is most certainly tired, worn out in fact; his constitution is not as strong as he would like. Nevertheless, we must press on.'

'Aye, you're no wrong. I'll pass your request on to my mother directly. Will ye follow on and come an' meet her?'

'And some food,' Albert added as Duncan turned away to cross the ford. 'A little food, my dear fellow, would be most appreciated.'

Duncan nodded and made his leave.

You shall be well rewarded. Those were the words Albert had said to them. He hoped the Prince stayed true to his promise.

* * *

'The Queen wants to meet you, *màthair*.'

Gail McAdie froze at the words. Duncan could not help chortling; perhaps it was a mean trick to play, but he could not resist. After the trials and stresses of the last few days he felt an urgent need to be a child again, even if just for one moment.

Gradually his mother's expression changed from frozen indecision to, briefly, mirth—before settling on what Duncan decided must be pious misery.

'Your father has told me the truth.'

McAdie emerged from behind the curtain, a cup of water in one hand, wiping stray droplets from his moustaches with the other. In the candlelight he cut a fearsome figure: all bristling beard and glinting eyes.

'What have you told her?' Duncan demanded.

'Only the truth. We're to pack our things. The Duke willnae let us stop here long.'

'But you dinnae ken that for sure!'

'The hunt failed, laddie. The Duke gave me a chance, and what have we done with it? Nothing!'

Duncan glanced at his mother. The poor woman was tidying and cleaning in a frenzy: rushing around the tiny interior of the cottage, stacking plates, dusting the top of the cupboards, tearing drying clothes off the line and bundling them out of sight. She emitted a sob but did not dare add to the conversation. The sound drove a spike through Duncan's heart.

His father made him so angry. Why did he always act the pessimist? Why could he never see the best in people, only assume the worst? Perhaps it was something to do with growing older and never quite achieving the success he felt he deserved; but whatever the cause, Duncan knew that this time he had to make a stand.

'You've given up! Look at what you achieved. You brought Albert to within thirty yards of the beastie, a perfect shot, aye? And after such a chase as songs are made of! *He* didnae pull the trigger; *you* did your job. The Duke will sing your praises when he hears.'

McAdie's eyes flashed. He tossed his cup to one side. It clattered against the stone wall of the lodge.

'Ye know nothing. It disnae matter what might've been. Only success or failure counts.'

The door banged. Duncan turned to see Queen Victoria standing on the step.

'What is the cause of this delay?'

* * *

The Queen held her lantern aloft to light her way. The light dazzled Duncan, and for a moment he was unable to see the details of her expensive clothes, only the outline of her form. She looked like any other weary mountain traveller: wet boots, muddy skirts, hair tied back in a practical bun.

Then she lowered her lantern, and Duncan's mother gasped. She set her broom down and gave an awkward curtsey. Duncan had never seen her so surprised.

'Your Majesty … I … och, I hope ye'll forgive the state o' my house…'

Victoria directed her stern gaze at the lady. 'May I come in?'

'Aye, please do … Have a seat.'

The Queen remained standing. She put her lantern down on the table, folded her arms, and glared at Duncan and his father.

'While you two argue, Ewan Carr may be dying. Have you forgotten that he needs urgent care?'

McAdie's scowl did not shift. He said nothing at all, but by the twitch in his left cheek Duncan could see the rage and frustration building up within him. Out there on the hunt he had overstepped the mark while addressing Prince Albert, forgetting himself for a few moments and speaking out of turn; fortunately the bond between forester and master could occasionally permit such lapses.

Would he also lash out at the Queen? Such a thing would not be forgiven. Duncan prayed that his father was able to control himself.

Victoria waited a moment, then raised an eyebrow at him and turned to address Duncan's mother instead.

'Since your husband has decided to be *unaccommodating*, perhaps you can help us. Has your son explained the situation?'

'No, your Majesty … Ma'am … he has been arguing wi' his father, I'm ashamed to say.' She looked at Duncan, and in her gaze he saw confusion and hurt. *Why can my family not be united and happy for once?*—he heard the question as clearly as if she had said it out loud.

'Well, no matter. A member of our group has been shot. He's just a boy. The wound is infected. Would you be kind enough to help?'

McAdie cleared his throat. He looked from his wife to the Queen. 'Ma'am, will ye allow me to speak for my wife? I must respectfully forbid it.'

'Why?'

'If we're to be evicted, she will be needed at home to pack our things.'

Gail McAdie frowned at her husband. It was a shy look, perhaps the beginnings of a revolution against McAdie's domineering influence over the family, but Duncan did not miss it. She collected herself and nodded at the Queen. Gail still seemed to be stupefied by the royal visit, but at last she had been given the chance to assert her own wishes for once instead of timidly obeying her husband in all things.

'I will do it,' she whispered, and reached out to take her son's hand. She seemed to draw strength from him, for when she spoke again her tone was confident and strong and she held her head higher than before. 'I'll help. Will ye stop here the night?'

'We must press on to Blair,' Victoria said. 'Much depends on it. Will you come with us and look after him?'

She smiled. 'Aye.'

Duncan was overjoyed that his mother, long resigned to a life of duty and obedience, had at last found the strength to assert herself and make a decision of her own. On the other hand, even if he did not agree with his father, he was able to understand his point of view. Ever the practical man, McAdie was at this present moment concerned with the thing that mattered most to him: his family's future. His behaviour may appear callous but he was motivated by love.

They packed what supplies they needed and set off on the road once again.

* * *

Forbes stumbled along in darkness.

The strange sense that the French called déjà-vu had crept over him gradually during the last few miles. He felt that he had done this before, trodden the same long road in the dark, plunged into the same bogs, stubbed his toe against the same stones lying wait in the mud. The sufferings of his body fogged the workings of his mind and it took him hours to recollect that he had passed this way before, travelling north instead of south; and, as before, they had tramped in darkness. The Queen's lantern had long since gone out.

Only a few days ago, but it feels like a year. Time is playing tricks on me.

He felt dreadfully thirsty, but could not seem to concentrate on the act of walking and summoning the words to ask for water at the same time. In contrast to the last time he had travelled through Glen Tilt, this time Duncan never left his side; on their journey north, he recalled, the young man had impatiently rushed on ahead, frequently leaving his ailing charge behind. Now he and his mother walked beside the pony which bore Carr, drugged and feverish, along the road.

'Not far now, sir,' Duncan would say every half an hour or so, ever cheerful. 'Think on the feather bed and hot meal at the end o' the journey.'

And my dear wife and children. Forbes thought of little else, when his mind would allow cogent thought at all.

His feet had become red hot stumps of agony. He focused on that pain. It drew his attention away from the other symptoms: the fog in his mind, the rat in his gut, the weakness in his limbs … the worry that paralysis and apoplexy would strike him down once again. Perhaps next time he would not wake up.

The road played games with his mind. Five miles passed by in seconds, then the next hundred yards seemed to last a month.

'Forest Lodge,' someone called out. 'Is anyone in residence? Wake the butler!'

'There'll be nobody in,' McAdie's voice replied. 'All the staff will be away at Bruar Lodge this week.'

They marched onwards.

* * *

With Albert's support, Victoria felt that she had managed the situation competently until now. She had fulfilled her promise to Alicia Forbes. She had believed Professor Balfour despite her initial unwillingness to accept his claims.

Happily Albert had realised of his own accord that the men he chased were not poachers at all. Yes, it had turned out rather well; it would have turned out a little better if Isaac had not shot poor Mr Carr, of course, but in general Victoria was rather pleased with how she had managed things. She was looking forward to her whole family being back under one roof again so they could enjoy what remained of their holiday.

However, all of her good work could be undone the moment the Duke once again became involved.

His displeasure could ruin everything. She and Albert counted him as a friend and, after all, he had been rather good to them over the years, lending them the use of his castle, extending them every possible courtesy and kindness, and going to considerable effort to make them feel as welcome as possible in Scotland. Their love of the Highlands would probably never have been kindled were it not for his labours.

Yet, for reasons altruistic or selfish, the Duke placed great importance on this particular visit. There would be accusations and recriminations. The McAdies would in all likelihood be blamed, and would suffer for this adventure, she was sure of it. Victoria was well aware that she owed a great deal to both the Duke and to the McAdies. Her skills of negotiation and mediation would be put to the test.

They finally reached the gates of Blair Castle a little after five o'clock in the morning. The dawn was a tranquil one. Victoria thought the watery blush of colour in the east would make a good subject for a painting, although no picture could capture the music of the dawn chorus.

Ordinarily the gates would be locked and unmanned at this o'clock, but for the duration of the royal visit every entrance to the castle grounds was guarded by Atholl Highlanders. Victoria was not entirely surprised to find one of them leaning against the wall with his head nodding against his chest. His companion jabbed him in the ribs and they both stood to attention as the column approached.

'Welcome back to Blair Atholl, your Majesty,' one of them said, after rubbing his eyes.

Victoria smiled at them. 'Good morning. Would you be good enough to wake the Duke?'

The guard saluted, and departed at a run up the long avenue that led to the castle.

* * *

The servants were already awake and about their duties at this hour, but it seemed to Victoria that they did not take kindly to this intrusion on their routine. Mr Samson, the butler, refused to allow any but Victoria and Albert through the front door.

'The others must wait in the servants' hall,' he insisted, politely but firmly. 'With respect, look at the state of them. The master would not allow it.'

Victoria turned to look at her fellow travellers. The two foresters were plastered in mud, standing with the uneven postures of men who had been marching for too long and sought some relief by transferring their weight from foot to foot. Alec McAdie's expression was perfectly neutral but Victoria had seen a glimpse of the resentment and anger that seethed beneath. The son, Duncan, merely looked exhausted.

They will not object to a cup of tea and some breakfast in the servants' hall, she thought, *but what about the Professor and his student? They are not of the servant class.*

Gail McAdie tended to the unconscious figure of Ewan Carr, wiping his forehead with a cloth and checking his pulse. She looked up and smiled. Victoria did not know the woman, but it was clear that she had found a sense of purpose in caring for the injured youth. McAdie seemed to be of the domineering variety of husband.

'I'll look after the boy downstairs,' Gail said. 'Dinnae worry about that. He's in no condition to be greetin' over such things.'

Victoria returned the butler's firm look with one of her own. 'Very well—the invalid shall join you in the servants' hall with the McAdies, but the Professor is coming with us into the house. I shall not be moved on this matter.'

Samson did not budge from the doorway of the castle. 'His Grace will not approve.'

She ignored him. 'Where is Isaac? When did he get back?'

'Get back, Ma'am? I thought he was with your party.'

He said the words with a straight face. Victoria examined his expression for signs of deceit, but could see none; on the other hand, butlers were very good at concealing their true emotions.

Annoyed, she glanced at Albert. 'Isaac has not yet returned with a doctor. Where could he have got to?'

Albert looked ill: pale, shaken by the exertion of the hunt, beaten down by the elements.

'I don't know, *mein Lieb*. Lately it seems that Isaac listens to me less than he used to.'

Once again Victoria called to mind her suspicions about Isaac. Why had he been the one to obey Murray's foolish order and shoot at the retreating form of Ewan Carr? Why had he refused to believe Professor Balfour, instead treating him like a criminal and chasing him out of the estate? And now, when a young man's life depended on his haste and efficiency, the Jaeger was nowhere to be found.

'I don't like him. When we return to England I want you to dismiss him from your staff.'

He shook his head. 'He is the best man I have hunted with. I won't part with him.'

She let it lie for now. There would be plenty of time later to adjust Albert's staff.

Samson stepped aside to allow the Duke to walk through the doorway and greet his visitors. Usually a man of not inconsiderable physical presence, on this occasion the effect was diluted by the green dressing-gown and slippers he was wearing. Victoria studied his expression carefully. Behind the frown and the knitted brows she detected anxiety—or perhaps fear.

Nevertheless, Murray stepped forward to embrace Albert.

'My friend … your Royal Highness! I am relieved beyond words that you are safe.'

Albert looked like he might be crushed by the Duke's bear-hug. 'I am most gratified by your concern. Alas, the hart eluded us.'

'That is to be regretted, but the mountains can be dangerous. When the storm blew in I feared the worst.' He stepped back and smiled, then turned to bow to Victoria. 'I regret the harsh words I said to you when we parted, Ma'am. I … I hope you can find it in your generous heart to forgive me.'

He scanned the weary travellers as he spoke, and Victoria understood the subtext of his words: *Was I right? Were the intruders poachers as I claimed?*

She smiled. 'All is forgiven. I hope you do not mind very much that I have invited some of the poachers back to the castle for rest and convalescence.'

Interestingly, the Duke paid hardly any attention to the figure of James Forbes, who had slumped against the wall sipping water from his flask. No: all his attention was focused on the unconscious youth on the pony's back. He pointed at Ewan Carr.

'Why have you brought that … that criminal to my house?'

'Because he was shot on your orders and is close to death. Where is the doctor? Has Isaac not returned with medical help?'

He ignored the question. 'Have the courtesy to remove Carr from my sight. I will not have him near me.'

Albert, who had been in a stupor since reaching journey's end, now came back to life. He frowned and strode up to the Duke, looked him in the eye. Now that he had found the strength to draw himself up to his full height, he did not look quite so frail compared to the Duke after all.

'How do you know that young man's name? I thought he was a mere poacher to you. What is happening here, Murray?'

The Duke fell silent. He gestured to his butler, who coughed and stepped forward on cue.

'Perhaps it is time to take the servants downstairs for some rest and breakfast. You have all walked a very long way. Surely the McAdies would rather be sitting in front of a warm fire than listening to the talk of their masters, hm?'

Victoria nodded without looking away from the Duke. 'Yes. That is a splendid idea. Be sure to take Ewan Carr with you and give Mrs McAdie whatever medical supplies you have.'

The Duke dared to meet her eyes for the first time during the course of the confrontation. His soul was riddled with guilt, she could feel it; but he did not dare to contradict her order.

Alec McAdie refused to move. He had the look of a desperate man. 'I'll not budge until I hear a word from the master. Your Grace, you promised me something if the hunt went well, aye?'

Murray's expression was ferocious when he looked at him. 'But the hunt did not go well, did it? Wait below. I shall deal with you and your son later.'

'But—'

'Be gone!'

Victoria directed what she hoped was a calming smile at the old forester. 'Do as I ask, McAdie. All will be well.'

As Samson led the McAdies away, Victoria wondered if she had just lied to them.

* * *

Duncan followed his mother and father downstairs to the servants' hall. After so long under the open sky he felt disoriented by the low ceilings and dark corridors of the castle's underbelly. Samson had ordered a pair of footmen to load Carr onto a handcart while Floraidh grazed the fresh grass in the garden. The poor lad bumped from side to side like a rag doll as the cart descended the ramp into the bowels of the castle.

'The Queen said there would be a doctor,' his mother whispered as they followed Samson to the heart of the servants' domain. 'I cannae save him alone, *beagan*. Look at the poor laddie.'

His face was pale, very pale, and had a wet gleam as if he sweated profusely. The drugs would wear off soon, his mother informed him; they were not strong, but she had nothing better.

McAdie grunted. 'He's in God's hands now.'

'If God is merciful then he'll be spared.' She cast a reproachful glance at her husband. 'Thank Heaven the boy's fate isnae in your hands, Alec.'

'Why blame me? I have to look after my family since nobody else has our interests in mind.'

Duncan recollected that his father had never been a soft-hearted man. He had never once betrayed an ounce of emotion at the death of a living creature, and as an estate forester he had seen his fair share of death.

Samson held the big double doors open and they stepped into the kitchens.

The first thing Duncan noticed was an ornate rifle laid on the kitchen table, trimmed with silver and gleaming in the firelight. The second thing he noticed was a Bavarian peaked hat hanging on a peg by the fireplace.

His father noticed it too. Both men stiffened, alert for any signs of the owner of those items.

'Isaac is here after all!' McAdie breathed. 'I dinnae trust him. He's at the heart of our misfortunes, I'd swear to it.'

After the handcart rolled through the doorway, Samson shut and locked the doors behind them. Duncan spun around.

Samson folded his arms and regarded them calmly. 'The master has left instructions that you are to remain here until summoned. Please make yourselves comfortable. There is tea in the pot and stew on the range. The lady will have access to the medicinal cabinet if she wishes to treat the invalid.'

'An' what if we wish to leave?' McAdie growled, right hand moving to the hilt of his knife.

'Please, McAdie. Sit and eat.' The old butler spread his palms in a pacifying gesture. 'Nobody downstairs wishes you any harm.'

Duncan noticed the slight emphasis Samson placed on the word *downstairs*. He glanced at his father, and by the murderous glint in his eye saw that he had not missed it either.

'Where is that bastard Isaac?'

'Upstairs, making arrangements for a transfer of his employment to the master of this house.'

The truth hit Duncan like a cannonball. *No!* Now he saw clearly the answer to the riddle, the meaning behind it all.

* * *

Victoria and Albert followed the Duke up the flight of stairs to the drawing room.

'I should like to see the children,' Albert said, then looked down at his dirty clothes. He laughed. 'And perhaps have a bath.'

She gripped his hand. 'As would I, dear, but we must do this first. Besides, the children will still be asleep.'

She looked back at the Professor. He had allowed a footman to take his muddy boots and give him some soft shoes to wear, but his feet must hurt terribly for he limped with every step. Something still appeared to cloud his senses for he hardly spoke, and when he looked at her it was as if through a veil of mist.

'Don't worry, Professor. You will see your wife and daughters again soon.'

'I should like that.'

When they reached the drawing room, Victoria was surprised to see Isaac standing by the fireplace, smoking a pipe and gazing out of the tall windows.

The Jaeger had a relaxed air this morning. He no longer wore his hunting clothes, but was dressed like any other country gentleman in breeches and morning coat. His moustache was freshly waxed. Victoria had never seen him with a waxed moustache before.

The glint in his eye was a dangerous one.

When Albert saw him, the vision fixed him to the spot where he stood; he swayed, and for a frightening moment Victoria thought he would fall until he rallied himself and stood up straight, regarding his servant with a look of disbelief and disappointment.

'Isaac ... *warum bist du hier?*'

Isaac smiled broadly. 'Good hunt, sir? No? Well, never mind. The Duke and I have an item of business to discuss with you.'

The Duke stood beside Isaac and briefly rested a hand on his shoulder. 'This man here has proven himself one of the finest damned huntsmen I have ever seen. I am in awe of his skills.'

Albert was shaking his head. 'He did not assist me on the hunt, Murray. Have you forgotten that I dismissed him after he shot Carr and chased away the hart? Isaac is a fine Jaeger, but on this occasion he has proven nothing except that he is unable to follow my orders.'

'But his interpretation of *my* orders, his execution of the command I gave him when you all arrived, has been masterful.'

Victoria thought she began to understand. Of course, it all made so much sense! Isaac's wilful behaviour, his uncharacteristic disregard for orders … he had been dancing to quite a different tune all along.

'What command?' she demanded.

'To prevent that whelp of a student from interfering with Albert's hunt.'

Professor Forbes, who had been standing quietly by the window watching the gardens, gave a discreet cough. All heads turned in his direction.

'You will forgive me if I find it difficult to speak at present, but I am not well.' He pulled a creased and waterlogged scrap of paper out of his inner coat pocket. 'I think perhaps I am in a position to explain. You ought to read this.'

Victoria accepted the letter, unfolded it, scanned the smudged lines written in haste on the mountain.

"The truth is that I am without a shilling. I own nothing but my clothes…"

"…My final defeat occurred one month ago when I played against the Duke of Atholl who is a member of my club … The villain refused to pay me back…"

"…Shots were fired on both sides…"

She closed her eyes and groaned. Now she understood. She passed the letter to Albert, and while he read it she was conscious of the Duke's gaze, hard and merciless, watching them both.

'He's a drinker, and he gets creative with the truth when intoxicated,' Murray said. 'Did you know that about him? Or anything about him whatsoever, in fact, before you both decided to pry into my affairs? Carr is a meddlesome little devil who has slandered my good name, attacked me, and done everything in his power to cause mischief.'

Albert folded the letter and gave it back to Forbes. He breathed in deeply and faced the Duke head on.

'Sir, you have been a good friend to us. My family owe you much. It was never our wish to *pry*, but certain things have occurred which no gentleman can permit himself to ignore. The shooting and harrying of men is one of those things—especially men whom to all appearances are innocent of any crime save trespass.'

'Yet you were quite willing to chase them when you thought they were poachers. Come now, we are both gentlemen; let us not pretend the term means anything more lofty than position in society. The moment you found out the men you chased were not low-born criminals you developed a conscience.' The Duke glanced at Forbes. 'I believe Professor Forbes has some family of rank, and Carr's background may be in trade but he is articulate and tolerably cultured, when he is sober at least.'

'Yet you were quite willing to order Isaac to shoot at them like fleeing wolves,' Victoria said as calmly as she could, barely able to contain her fury. 'That is not how the nobility conducts itself in my kingdom.'

'With respect, this is Scotland. We do things differently here. Besides, the boy tried to kill me! Does he say *that* in his note, by God?'

'Who fired the first shot?' she asked.

'Does it matter? His gang waylaid me beside the Tilt days before you arrived: Carr, that stubborn blackguard Balfour, and a few others. They were rather heavily armed for a botanical expedition. Now do you see why I have taken steps to secure my estate for the safety of my distinguished guests?' He ran a hand through his hair. 'Think of the scandal if any harm had befallen you.'

Albert waved a hand impatiently. 'What does this have to do with my Jaeger?'

Isaac glanced at the Duke for permission to speak. The Duke, who had worked himself up into a fury, seemed to be glad of the pause. He nodded his approval, and Isaac spread his hands wide in a pacifying gesture.

'There was a bargain. We knew Carr's gang were somewhere in Glen Tilt. I was to break them up and stop them interfering with the hunt, and in return the Duke promised to take me on as head keeper of the estate.'

Nobody spoke for a moment. This revelation stunned the royal couple to silence. Victoria gripped her husband's hand, could feel him trembling even as he stared at Isaac, shocked to the core of his being.

'Did you not think to discuss this with me first? Are you unhappy in my employment?'

For the first time Isaac had the grace to look a little ashamed. 'I was very happy with you, Albert … once. I was the best Jaeger in Bavaria. Now I hunt but a few times a year when your household decides to go to the country! It is no life for a man such as me. Estate life is what I wish for myself.'

'If you had only told me before! Now a young man may be dying. It is clear to me that I am to blame.'

Albert's words were full of regret. Victoria's heart ached for him. 'No, dearest, no … it is not your fault. Murray, Isaac does not deserve to be head keeper, but I know a man who does deserve that position—a man who has served you well and faithfully for many years, who has demonstrated his skills in every possible way, who has kept Albert alive in the mountains despite everything.'

'Ha! You speak of the old dog McAdie. He has had his day. I need younger and more ambitious stock if I am to make my estate a success.'

'He is a better Jaeger than Isaac,' Albert pressed. 'He brought me within yards of Damh-mor on two occasions after a chase of many miles. Never before have I seen such skills. And he's tough! You are a fool to cast aside such a man.'

'But he failed. His family will leave my employment as I promised they would if he did not do his duty.'

'*Verdammt*, man, the fault was mine!' Albert shouted, striking his fist against the red wallpaper. 'Will you not see reason?'

Victoria had never heard Albert curse before. She gasped—both at the shock of the word and at the intensity with which he was fighting for McAdie.

The Duke was unmoved. 'I will thank you not to raise your voice in my home. You may be royalty, but you are still my guests, and if I had not extended my hand in friendship to you I doubt you would have come to Scotland at all.'

Victoria studied them both, the Duke and his new estate keeper, standing next to the fireplace, poised and in control despite the stress of the argument. They had readied themselves for this confrontation days ago, she realised, and in that moment she knew that she and Albert could not win.

'Come on, my dear. It is enough. Let us go and talk to the McAdies.'

Albert looked heartbroken when he turned towards her. 'I don't know what to say to him. *Mein Gott*, Victoria, I feel like a villain. I made him a promise.'

'Hush, now. All will be well. Professor Forbes, would you be kind enough to come with us? I think our business here is concluded.'

* * *

Duncan waited with his family. They could do nothing more until they were summoned.

With the aid of the medicinal cabinet, Carr seemed to be doing a little better. His wound had been properly cleaned, washed with neat alcohol, dressed with a clean bandage, and elevated. He now moaned in his sleep and writhed in pain, a sure sign (according to Duncan's mother) that the narcotic drug was starting to wear off.

McAdie's rage had calmed. Now he squatted on a stool by the oven, gulping tea and shovelling stew into his mouth. He did not speak, but from time to time directed a belligerent look at the young footman who had been charged with the task of making sure they did not leave the kitchen.

Duncan was too tired to protest. He pulled his boots off at the earliest opportunity to inspect the damage. He spent most of his life on foot, and was used to walking twenty five miles a day; consequently, the soles of his feet were tough as rawhide. Nevertheless, the skin of both heels was stripped and raw, and an ugly blister lurked on each big toe.

Half an hour elapsed before anyone from upstairs came to see them. When the door opened, all heads turned to see who it could be.

It was the royal couple.

Victoria glanced at the footman, who touched his forelock and withdrew, closing the kitchen door behind him. Albert looked about the kitchen with a calculating air. Duncan had heard that the Prince paid great attention to the efficient management of the royal palace, and that he had an eye for laggardliness and corruption among servants. No doubt he had been keeping a mental record of everything he saw during his stay at Blair Atholl.

Silently, Albert drew a chair for himself and sat down at the head of the kitchen table. His expression was indeterminable. He looked at nobody and said nothing. At this point Duncan would give a great deal to know precisely what had been discussed upstairs.

His father fixed the Prince with a stare at once piercing and hopeful, an interrogative look, all seething emotion, a conflict between relief and despair; he did not know which yet to choose.

Victoria remained standing and looked at each member of the McAdie family in turn. She appeared poised, regal, in control of the situation.

'It is our unhappy duty to tell you that the Duke of Atholl wishes to terminate your employment, and that therefore you are required to give up the tenancy of Lochain Lodge in a period of one week. However—'

Duncan's father, who had sat utterly still while Victoria began her speech, now emitted a strangled cry and leapt to his feet.

'No! Tell me it isnae true!' He turned his wild eyes on Prince Albert. 'You … you swore ye'd speak for us. An' for a wee while I thought you were better than the rest. The ruling class is all the same, and to hell wi'ye all!'

Albert met his gaze. He looked almost as tortured as McAdie, but unlike the forester he remained calm and composed. Only the awful regret in his eyes betrayed the truth.

'I spoke for you, McAdie. We both spoke for you. I am only sorry it did not convince your master.'

Duncan was horrified to find that he felt only a heady sense of freedom at this news. It is a profoundly curious thing to feel an entire future self crumbling to dust in the space of a few moments: years of life disintegrating and dispersing on the winds of change. He had never felt anything like it. Until now, every moment of his life had been much the same as the one before it. His world was one of slow change and his destiny had been mapped out from the day of his birth. He had learned the skills of his father's trade, and he would be a forester until the day he died.

Until now…

This is it. This is the moment I have been waiting for. This is my chance to begin the life I choose for myself, instead of the life chosen for me.

His mother's sobs jolted him out of his selfish reverie. Life, of course, could never be that simple.

She wrung the corner of the tablecloth between her hands, and the look in her eyes was one of bottomless despair. Duncan had never known the uncertainty and misery of unemployment, but his mother and father had both spent dark years out of work and starving. The ladder climbing from that depth back into the light was a long and tortuous one, and Duncan knew that at their time of life they had no wish to make that journey a second time.

'What will we do? Where will we go?'

McAdie now stood behind his wife's chair and embraced her bony shoulders, hugging her body to his, both offering and receiving comfort in that difficult moment. She let go of the tablecloth and gripped his arms as if fearing he would let go.

Duncan could not remember the last time he had seen a tender embrace between his parents. The moment made him shed a tear at the pity of it: that it had taken an event this cataclysmic to bring the family closer together once again, for his father to finally see beyond his introspection and his temper to realise that looking after his family was more than a purely practical task.

Victoria wrung her hands together, visibly affected by the distress her words had caused.

'My dear people, do not despair so! You did not let me finish what I have to say.'

McAdie shook his head. 'It was enough. I cannae think of anything you might say that would bring us any comfort.'

'What if I were to say that we are thinking of purchasing our own estate? Albert, you tell him.'

The beginnings of understanding flickered in McAdie's eyes as he perceived what the royal couple might be about to offer.

Albert raised his hand with a gesture intended to encompass the Atholl estate. 'I have observed much during my visits to Blair. Victoria and I love the Highlands so, but this visit has proven that there can be ... complications when visiting an estate owned by someone else, even if the owners are friends.' Here he gave a wry smile. 'I am at my happiest when in the wild. It reminds me of my youth. You and I have much common ground, McAdie.'

'Aye, we are both men o' the hills.'

'And that is why Victoria and I have decided to purchase an estate. We shall, of course, require a head keeper to manage our deer forest. You are the man for the job. What do you say?'

For a moment McAdie did not respond. He simply stared at Albert with an open mouth. Then: 'When estates are bought, the auld keeper stays in his position. He kens the land. It isnae done to bring in new men.'

Victoria shook her head.

'We want *you*, McAdie, and your entire family shall find employment with us. That is our solemn promise, and in addition to this pledge—which we naturally cannot fulfil immediately, as we have not even selected an estate to buy—it is our intention to make a gift of fifty pounds to you in recognition of the services you have rendered to us during the course of our stay.' She smiled at Duncan. 'Your son shall also receive twenty five pounds.'

Duncan gasped. Twenty five pounds! The sum was inconceivable to him. He had never had more than a few shillings in his pocket at once, plus a few more hidden behind a loose stone in Lochain Lodge. What could he do with twenty five pounds? Suddenly the world seemed very bright and full of promise.

McAdie strode over to Albert's end of the table and shook his hand vigorously. It might have been a trick of the light, but Duncan thought he saw a tear glint in his father's eye.

'God bless you, sir. You are a good man after all.'

Albert looked exceedingly pleased with himself. 'When I make a promise it is not done lightly. I said you would be rewarded when the adventure was over, and rewarded you shall be.'

Duncan uttered a prayer of thanks. His parents would be saved—would, in fact, be made prosperous. He could leave and pursue the life he wanted with a clean conscience.

* * *

Professor Forbes took his leave of Blair Atholl quietly.

His continued presence here was of little moment. He mattered little to the royals and nobles who had invested so much in the Atholl expedition; even the estate foresters, hard-working mountain folk for whom he had nothing but the greatest of respect, were purely concerned with the outcome and aftermath of the great hunt. Victoria and Albert had no doubt forgotten about him the moment they left the drawing room. He had overheard a footman gossiping with the ladies' maid and ascertained that the Queen had made an extravagant gift to the McAdies. Well, good luck to them; they deserved it for their heroic efforts, but he had no doubt that they too would have forgotten all about the quiet Professor with whom they had travelled for a while.

He rather liked the fact that the "wee beastie" continued to roam free, wearied and wounded by the persistent attacks of his human aggressors, perhaps, but very much alive.

The mountains have had the last word this time. They often do.

Without telling anyone what it contained, he had left an envelope with Albert's valet, to be opened after he was gone. In it he had included a letter explaining that Ewan Carr was to receive the best medical and legal aid available, and all bills were to be sent to the Edinburgh residence of Professor James Forbes. He could not leave without knowing that his foolish student would be safe. He doubted that Carr would be permitted to stay at Blair after everything that had transpired, but at least he would be looked after—and would have the help he required to fight for the money he was owed by the Duke.

He smiled as he strode down the avenue towards the castle gatehouse. The morning was a calm one, the countryside quiet except for the background music of a thousand songbirds. The rounded dome of a mountain peak appeared above the trees for a tantalising moment before he walked on and the view was obscured once more. The light had an ethereal quality to it, as if it shone from another world into this.

Pain lanced into his side. The dappled green of the gardens wheeled around his head, and he dropped to his knees, gasping for air.

I am paying for my adventure. Alicia, I hope you will forgive me…

He heard running feet. Someone cradled his head and shouted 'Fetch a carriage, and be quick about it!'

* * *

When he awoke, the first thing he perceived was his wife's face.

Sunlight streamed through the window and illuminated loose strands of her hair in an angelic halo. Her eyebrows were creased with worry but hope blossomed in her eyes as she saw that her husband was conscious. Her lips parted and she uttered a sigh.

Some aspect of her had changed since he had seen her last. She looked older, perhaps … no, not older; merely more careworn.

'Hello, wife,' he said, and all of a sudden the emotions he had been keeping buried deep within him burst to the surface and overflowed.

He closed his eyes and strove to remain calm. His body trembled, violently at first, until he felt Alicia grip his hand. Gradually, calm returned, and he gazed back up at her again.

'How are the children?'

'They have asked about you almost every hour of every day. You could not be a greater hero to them. Their papa, the gallant mountain explorer!' She traced a finger down his unshaven cheek. 'You have lost weight.'

He nodded, waiting silently for the recriminations to begin. He deserved everything she chose to throw at him.

For a while she said nothing, wearing a patient smile he had seen so many times before. After a few moments the smile changed subtly and he perceived that she was not angry with him after all.

'You can be a difficult man to live with at times, James. Sometimes I question why I married you. Hush! Don't say anything until I have finished.' She laid a finger on his lips. 'When I read your book on the Alps I didn't understand any of it … rocks and ice and a hundred claims that seem to rebel against everything the Bible teaches us. What could that matter? I saw your work as a wedge driven between us.'

'It need not be so,' he began, but she stopped him with a stern look.

'Do you wish to know what changed my mind?'

He nodded.

'Duncan McAdie brought you here. When he speaks of you it is in the same way a follower speaks of a prophet. Do you know what loyalty you have inspired in that young man? Do you realise how you have changed the way he looks at the world?'

In truth, he had no idea. Duncan was not as taciturn as his father, but his true feelings were no less opaque.

'You have inspired him,' Alicia continued. 'Perhaps in your own way you are a prophet. You seek something out there in the wild, I realise that now; something you cannot find at home, and without which your soul cannot thrive.' She shook her head and smiled. 'I may worry dreadfully while you are out there, but I think you will be remembered for what you do.'

'I have done nothing. I went looking for a glacier but was woefully unprepared for what I found. I made no measurements worthy of scientific attention. My expedition has been a complete failure.'

'But you dared to try, despite my pleas and despite the danger. That is worth something, surely?'

He took a moment to absorb what she was saying to him. Alicia had never understood or approved of his work, he had accepted that long ago; and yet now, when he deserved every word of criticism, she seemed to have found some meaning in what he did after all.

'Even though I have nearly killed myself?'

She cradled his head. 'By the grace of God or by your own good judgement, I know not which, you are alive. You will recover. I would try to make you promise not to do it again, but I know you cannot keep such a promise.'

That gentle smile again. Alicia had a great capacity for strength and fortitude, but he had never before seen this calm acceptance of his misdeeds.

'You are right. I cannot promise I won't do it a second time, but something has changed—that I *can* promise. I won't be motivated by pride ever again. I will conduct the work of science for its own sake, explore the mountains for the joy of being among them, and enjoy everything life can give me while I have the strength to do it. I may be ill, but by God I can still be the man I am meant to be.'

He had never meant anything more earnestly.

Life, for him, was a race to do and experience everything possible in the short span between the two oblivions all men must face. Alicia was part of that life, just as he was part of hers; but he would not and could not compromise the greater part of his being to prevent her worrying about his safety. How glad he was that she finally understood that fundamental truth about his soul.

Life is not safety. Life is cold and danger, terror and triumph, work and perseverance, high reward and the risk of utter ruin; it is the wind on the heights, the enchanting sunrise over the loch, the cry of a buzzard and the thunder of an avalanche; it is the first wail of your newborn child and the certain knowledge of your own mortality. The true gift is the knowledge that life is fleeting and there to be lived at all costs.

She interlocked her fingers with his, and her smile told him that she understood. 'How glad I am to hear you say it. I have not heard the name Agassiz mentioned since you came back to me.'

'That feud is over. I am my own man now.'

* * *

Forbes awoke gradually, marvelling at the absence of pain.

He lay there on the lawn without opening his eyes, enjoying the sounds of a summer afternoon in the Highlands: the music of a bumblebee, the distant complaints of cattle, the laughter of his children in the house. He breathed in the fragrance of heather.

When he opened his eyes, the pain did not return.

Duncan McAdie sat on the bench in the shade of the apple tree. Forbes studied him for a moment before sitting up. The youngster was gazing up at the top of the nearby Dunfallandy Hill, barely a thousand feet above their heads. Silhouettes of individual trees could be made out clearly against the blue sky. This hill was not capped by ice, was not rugged or rocky, had no distinguishing features of any kind; it was, in fact, just like a thousand other hills in Scotland.

Forbes had learned that Highlanders paid no attention to the hills themselves beyond practical concerns of how to travel from place to place while expending the least amount of energy—or, at most, how to use high points for watching the stags. Yet the expression on Duncan's face was one of distracted reverie as his eyes scanned the bumps and hollows of the wooded ridge above.

Forbes sat up and rubbed his eyes. He felt much better after his sleep, but knew that it would take weeks to recover. *This was supposed to be a restful holiday. I suppose I had better take my wife's advice and rest…*

Duncan rose from the bench.

'How d'ye feel, Professor?'

'A little better.' He rubbed his stomach. It felt severely bruised, as it often did after a bout of illness. 'I am much obliged to you, my boy. My wife tells me you brought me here after I collapsed.'

He shrugged, as if the long journey from Blair Atholl was nothing at all to be thanked for. 'Someone had to do it.'

'Someone had to save the foolish ailing professor from himself, you mean?' Forbes said with a smile. 'I suppose you think me comical … the under-prepared tourist losing himself in the mountains and falling prey to the weather.'

'At least I was there to help ye, in the end anyway.' Duncan looked awkward. 'I'd like to properly apologise for what I did at the Falls of Tarf. It was wrong of me to leave you. Can we part as friends?'

Forbes nodded. That meant a lot to him. He had suffered as a result of Duncan's duplicity, of that there could be no doubt; and yet he could not bring himself to condemn the lad for what he had done. Life in the mountains was tough—he had learned that the hard way—and Duncan had merely taken an opportunity when it had presented itself.

'I accept your apology. Thank you.'

He took a seat on the bench next to the young ghillie. They sat in silence for a while, looking up at the interplay of sunshine and shadow on the hill.

'Will ye come back to our mountains?' Duncan said at length.

'Perhaps. I may have found my glacier, but I have no evidence that it exists, and no real scientist would put forward a theory without evidence.'

Duncan nodded confidently. 'Ye'll be back.'

Will I? Perhaps I shall be dead in a year. Perhaps the mystery of Bràigh Riabhach will never be solved.

That thought made him sombre, until he looked up at the hill again and reflected that perhaps the answers meant nothing at all. The data tabulated by scientists in their ledgers is recorded without any trace of the pain or the effort required to collect it. Theories are barren without the glint of sun on snow or the whisper of spindrift in a crevasse. For it is not the answers which matter, or even the questions, but the fact that man is brave enough to voyage into untamed nature and ask his questions of a hostile world. That which truly matters is eternal and will never fade.

The act of exploration goes beyond science and into the sublime.

In time, when everything that can be known about the mountain realm has already been discovered and recorded by the long dead, humanity will still come back to these places, gaze into the sunrise, and ask their questions of the wild. The mountains will still be there, and new generations will find their own meanings in the storm and the silence of great heights.

'We are on the verge of a new dawn,' Forbes whispered. 'I don't know if it will come in my lifetime, or even yours, my boy, but mark my words; it's coming. Do you think about the future?'

'I think about nothing else,' Duncan said fervently.

'A time shall come when people flock to the Highlands in their thousands purely for the joy of climbing, and local men shall become wise and prosperous mountain guides. Make yourself and your family ready for that time, Duncan.'

Duncan looked up at the hill again, his expression thoughtful. 'Aye, Professor. I may stay in the Mounth a wee while yet. I may have the money I need to make a new start, but it's harder to leave than I thought it would be.'

Forbes smiled. 'And I find it harder to leave the mountains every time I visit them. It is the tragedy of my condition.' He coughed, and reached into his breast pocket for a card, which he gave to Duncan. 'My address. If you ever require employment, write to me. Don't forget, now! I might need your services as a guide a second time.'

Duncan traced the words on the card with a finger as he read. 'Will ye be well enough to travel again?'

'Nothing could prevent me. I may not get all the answers I want from the mountains before the end, but I will never stop asking my questions.'

* * * * *

THE END

WHAT NEXT?

This is the first book in the Alpine Dawn series. To receive an early email notification when Book II is published, sign up to my new release mailing list here: http://eepurl.com/u6PE1

If you have enjoyed this book and want to do your bit to help support the author, please consider leaving a review on Amazon and Goodreads. It takes only a few minutes but can have a dramatic impact, and might even help others to discover my work.

Tell people about this book! Post on Facebook, let Twitter know, spread the news face to face. Authors thrive on word of mouth.

The adventure doesn't have to end here. You might enjoy my novel, *The Only Genuine Jones*, a tale of adventure set in the mountains of Britain and the Alps in 1897. If you would prefer something shorter, *Crowley's Rival* takes the reader to the crags of the Lake District long before the days of guidebooks and safety equipment. Both titles are available on Amazon.

Visit my website:

www.alexroddie.com

Say hello on Twitter:

twitter.com/alex_roddie

Find me on Facebook:

www.facebook.com/alexroddiewriter

Turn the page to find out more about the history behind *The Atholl Expedition.*

HISTORICAL NOTES

The Atholl Expedition is fictional, but in common with my other books it is built on a core of truth.

In 1847, the Atholl estate was indeed owned by Sir George Murray, the 6th Duke of Atholl. He was involved in a notorious access battle that year, precipitated by the "Battle of Glen Tilt" on the 21st of August in which John Hutton Balfour and a number of students attempted to access Glen Tilt from the north. They were repulsed and harried by the Duke and his foresters, and Balfour, incensed by the treatment he had received, fought for a right of way through the reserve.

I have embellished and modified this event for narrative purposes, inventing the volatile character of Ewan Carr and his business dispute with Murray. I must stress that there is no evidence the Duke ordered shots to be fired at the intruders, although there's no doubt that he fought hard to prevent general access to Glen Tilt in the legal battle that followed.

Murray lost when the case went to court in 1850, and this outcome led to the formation of the Scottish Rights of Way Society.

The subsequent "Battle of Tarf Water" described in Chapter III is entirely fictional. There is no evidence that Balfour or his companions went back through Glen Tilt a second time.

Queen Victoria and Prince Albert visited Blair on several occasions over the years and were friends with the Duke and Duchess of Atholl. In August 1847 they were staying at Ardverikie, and were actually invited by the Duke to stay at Blair again, but Victoria declined the invitation as she wished to visit other areas of the Highlands.

I have tried to describe the relationship between Victoria and Albert as faithfully as possible. Their marriage was a largely harmonious one by 1847, although they had been locked in a power struggle years before and still fought on occasion—particularly if Albert went against the will of his wife. He loved to hunt but was not a very good shot, and during their first visit to Blair the Duke arranged for him to shoot tame deer in the gardens from the window of his room!

The royal family travelled with a number of servants, and that staff included Albert's faithful valets and Jaegers. The character of Isaac is entirely fictional and has no connection with any historical figure.

Professor James Forbes is one of my favourite figures from this period in the history of mountaineering. Tireless, prolific, yet suffering from a chronic illness that frequently prevented him from going into the field, Forbes was a pioneer in the science of glaciology. His epic survey of the Mer de Glace in 1842 helped to establish the basic facts of how and why glaciers move downhill. Forbes visited the Alps at a time when the mountains were largely unexplored and the maps were crude, but his scientific work paved the way for the great wave of mountaineering that was to follow.

The feud with Louis Agassiz (in which each accused the other of stealing his work) tainted his reputation in the 1840s and may even have contributed to the breakdown of his health. Not just an Alpine explorer, Forbes was a dedicated mountaineer in his native land of Scotland and climbed many of the peaks that would later become known as Munros. His achievements include the first recorded ascent of Sgurr nan Gillean with Duncan Macintyre in 1836. He completed a survey of Ben Nevis in 1847 and noted the impressive banks of semi-permanent snow clinging to its north face. In his many walks through the mountains Forbes pondered the question of prehistoric Scottish glaciers.

His work was not limited to the geography of mountains and glaciers, however. He applied his prodigal scientific mind to many branches of physics, and his achievements include the invention of the seismometer in 1842 and pioneering experiments into the conduction of heat.

There is no evidence that a genuine glacier existed in the upper corries of Braeriach (Bràigh Riabhach) in 1847. In the present day, An Garbh-choire is the site of the most persistent semi-permanent snow patches in Scotland, and it is not unreasonable to suppose that, considering the harsher winters of the 1840s and evidence of snow persisting throughout the year on much lesser hills, these remote Cairngorm icefields may have been extensive and seamed with glide cracks. The rumour of a surviving Scottish glacier is exactly the sort of thing James Forbes would have wanted to investigate.

As for the legends of the Bodach of Mar and Damh-mor, I have invented these for the purpose of my story. However, the Gaelic folklore of the Cairngorms was rich and varied at this time, and many glens and mountains had witches, monsters, or ghosts associated with them. It was commonly believed that certain stags were as wise as men and lived for hundreds of years.

I have written this story as a glimpse into the state of mountaineering culture in Scotland in the 1840s: a time before mountaineering culture really existed, and yet in the complex interactions of laird and forester, royalty and stag, student and Professor, science and superstition, we can begin to see the shadow of a future world taking shape. These are the days before people climbed the Munros for fun—indeed, Sir Hugh Munro had not even been born—and the Highlands were almost completely unknown to the tiny but growing class of sportsmen who saw mountains as sources of enjoyment and healthy exercise.

In 1847 the great revolution in mountain climbing was just around the corner. In the subsequent volumes of the Alpine Dawn series I will dramatise that process of change and bring it to life. However, although the Alps may have been ripe for exploration by the 1840s, the Highlands would in many ways remain obscure for much longer. As late as the 1870s it is possible that some Scottish peaks remained unclimbed, and it wasn't until the 1890s that Munro's List of 3000ft Peaks heralded a great wave of hillwalking for pleasure.

GLOSSARY OF TERMS

Aigeach – Stallion.

Alpenstock – Spiked staff used by mountaineers for support on steep slopes. Sometimes combined with an iceman's hatchet to form an ice axe.

Barraman – Snow cornice; an overhang of snow and ice that builds up on the edge of a cliff and can present a hazard.

Bergschrund – A large crevasse which often forms between a glacier and the upper slopes of a mountain.

Beagan – Little one.

Bealach – A col or saddle between two mountains.

Beinn – Mountain.

Bothy – A small hut or cottage, usually not used as a permanent habitation.

Burn – A small watercourse.

Corrie – A deep glen, often bowl-shaped, carved by glacial action in the prehistoric past.

Damh-mor – The great hart.

Dinnae fash yerself – Don't trouble yourself.

Donnered – Exhausted.

Eigh-shruth – Glacier.

Fàilte dhachaidh – Welcome home.

Feart – Afraid.

Feasgar math – Good evening.

Forester – Outdoor estate servant whose chief duties include acting as a hunting guide or attendant.

Ghillie – A man or boy who attends someone on a hunting or fishing expedition. In the 1840s the term was usually understood to mean a junior forester or forester's assistant.

Glissade – The act of sliding down a steep snowslope, usually on foot or sitting down. The descent may be controlled with a staff or ice axe.

Gralloching – The act of disembowelling a deer.

Halò – Hello.

Jaeger – German hunting guide or attendant.

Ken – Know.

Laird – Generic term for landowner or master.

Màthair – Mother.

Muckle – Large or big.

Shieling – Seasonal mountain dwelling.

Sgian-dubh – Small knife worn as part of traditional Highland dress.

Uisge-beatha – Whisky.

ACKNOWLEDGEMENTS

I would like to thank the following people for their support and help.

Firstly, my partner Hannah. This is not the first but the second obsession in book form she has helped me to complete, and every word I have written is for her.

Catherine Speakman has astonished me with the quality of her illustrations. I'm in awe of the skill with which she has interpreted my ideas and brought my characters to life.

Susan Fletcher, my friend and mentor, deserves a special mention for her kindness and guidance.

My editor, Clare Danek, has done a fine job of correcting and adjusting my unpolished prose.

A big hello also to the staff of the Coffee Bean, Skegness. I wrote much of this book in your cafe and have always found it a friendly and welcoming establishment.

Many other people have helped out in many ways, by giving advice on historical or linguistic matters, reading draft manuscripts, or assisting me with spreading the word about the new release. In particular I'd like to thank Robert Mayer (the talent behind the inimitable Prince Albert Twitter account @Albert_PrinceC), Joe Dorward, John Burns, Kath Middleton, Roddy John Murray, my parents Ian and Anita Roddie, Rachel Adams, Isi Oakley, Chris Highcock, Paul Wilkinson, the members of the UK Kindle Users Forums, the staff of Blair Castle, and every one of my Twitter followers who has commented on or retweeted one of my blog posts.

Lastly, my greatest thanks must go to the mountain that inspired this story. I have attempted to climb Braeriach five times but succeeded only twice. While such places still exist in the world, tales like this will have meaning.

BIBLIOGRAPHY

I have relied on a number of books during the research phase of writing this novel, and I believe they will be of interest to anyone wishing to study the subject further. Here are a few of the best.

Forbes, J. D. (1843), *Travels Through the Alps of Savoy and Other Parts of the Pennine Chain*, Adam and Charles Black. This is the epic story of Forbes' Alpine voyage of 1842. I commend this book to anyone with an interest in the history of mountaineering. More than just a record of scientific endeavour, it is an incredible adventure story in its own right and Forbes brings to life the Alpine world of the mid-19th century with considerable skill.

Kerr, J. (1993), *Life in the Atholl Glens*, Perth and Kinross Libraries. This is the definitive volume on the history of the Atholl glens, and contains many fascinating insights into the 6th Duke and his estate. It also includes the most complete account of the Battle of Glen Tilt I have been able to find.

Kerr, J. (1992), *Queen Victoria's Scottish Diaries*, Lochar Publishing. Victoria kept a diary almost every day of her life, and the contents of those diaries provide fascinating reading for their insights into the Scottish landscape and people. John Kerr's analysis introduces context and perspective.

Dorward, J. (2011), *Lowdown on the Upland of Mar*, Joe Dorward. This slim volume is a field guide to the glens and hills of the Mar forest. It goes beyond the average hillwalking guide in furnishing the reader with a wealth of historical and linguistic information about the landscape.